THE RIDDLE
OF THE
DUNES

a gripping historical murder mystery that keeps you guessing

JAMES ANDREW

THE
BOOK
FOLKS

Paperback published by The Book Folks

London, 2019

© James Andrew

ISBN 978-1-6945-2892-6

www.thebookfolks.com

For Duncan

CHAPTER ONE

When I returned from the war, things looked simple with no barbed wire to crawl under, no Germans to fight, no shells to avoid, and no bullets to duck. I strolled along civvy street, dressed in my demob suit and feeling like a king – if a badly dressed one. The suit was made of shoddy material and was so poorly sewn it felt ready to unravel at any moment, and it did after a few days. Then I had to use some of my small store of money to clothe myself properly. But the war was over, I told myself. That was what mattered. At least I thought it was – except, when I went to bed, it started all over again in my head and I woke screaming every night.

I don't know why I killed that young woman on the beach. I do remember her body lying on the sand with that gash in her head and the rock I'd used just beside her. They say anger is all consuming and they are right. The person I once was no longer exists.

I remember the flame of her hair as it caught the setting sun and the redness of the blood seeping out of her, and, as her life left her body, something left mine. Unfortunately, not the anger. Was it recognition of myself?

So, I went away. When I think back, it was the rage I was trying to escape. I travelled in random directions, trying to stamp down the fury with each step away. I tramped mile after mile each day hoping that my weariness would tire out that scream for violence in me, but it didn't work. I realised I was no longer myself. The anger had become me.

And that was when I found my feet had taken me back.

* * *

Daphne picked up the lead from the sideboard, the dog jumped at her with enthusiasm, and she found herself fobbing him off. As she clipped the lead onto the collar, she ruffled the hair on his head with her hand.

'Don't go anywhere near the Ridges,' Marion said to her. 'There are plenty of other places to take that dog.'

'The man who did those murders is gone,' Daphne replied to her mother. 'Everybody says so.'

'Always assume the worst,' Marion replied. 'It's safer that way.'

An impatient frown was on Daphne's face. 'You don't need to fret. I won't go there,' she said. 'But if that worries you, why don't you get Robert to do his own dog duty?'

'He does his best,' Marion replied.

'Have you any idea where Robert is?' Daphne asked.

'At Helen's, I expect. You should be more patient with him. He's had his problems,' Marion said.

'Don't we all know it?'

Pooky pulled at the lead. He had no time for arguments like these. Pooky was a mixture between a spaniel and something else. As he was not pure bred, no one had docked his tail, which now wagged its splendid plume hopefully. He was a young dog, only two years old, healthy and robust, of attractive colouring being brown-and-white, but neither Marion nor Daphne were paying attention to him. They stared accusingly at each other.

Marion was a broad-faced, robust-looking woman and, as this was her kitchen and her home, she was used to acting like the mistress of it. Though Daphne was, like her mother, a curly-headed brunette, her physical type was different. There was a slenderness about her figure that had probably never been there in Marion Tanner. When she argued with her mother, there was a querulousness in her voice, but her face looked just as defiant.

'It's supposed to be Robert's job to take Pooky for his walk today,' she replied.

Another voice entered the fray. This came from a middle-aged man who had been sheltering behind a newspaper. He put it down as he said, 'You were the one who nagged to get the dog in the first place.'

Slightly built like Daphne, but with thinning fair hair, and a tiredness in his face, this was her father, Pete Tanner. Daphne turned her eyes to meet his. 'Don't I know it?' she said. 'You remind me all the time.' Then she turned back to her mother. 'I'm just back from working in the shop. Don't I get five minutes to myself?'

'You've had something to eat and a natter with your mother.' Pete's voice spoke with weight, which further annoyed Daphne.

'I don't know why I'm agreeing to take the dog. Frank said he might call.'

'We'll send him after you,' Pete said.

'I don't understand why you bother with Frank,' added Daphne's mother.

'You used to think well enough of him,' Daphne told her.

'Used to is right,' Marion replied. 'Half the neighbours don't speak to me because of him.'

Aware of the familiar territory that an argument about taking the dog for a walk was heading towards, Daphne considered her reply. 'The half that are worth talking to still do,' she said. 'There's nothing wrong with Frank.'

Pete's voice now took on an appeasing tone. 'I like Frank myself,' he said. 'A well set-up and fine, principled man. Educated too. But it's an awful pity he became a conchie. I used to enjoy a banter with Albert next door. Now he cuts me dead. I know what your mother means.'

An image came into Daphne's mind of Albert's leering looks. She was glad relations with him had become distant. 'At least Frank's got manners,' Daphne muttered.

'What do you mean by that?' her father said.

'Nothing,' Daphne replied.

'Frank's lucky we make him welcome here,' Marion said.

'It's good of you,' Daphne said, but her voice suggested otherwise.

'Our Robert was willing to fight out there. Why was Frank too good to do that?' Daphne noticed the way her mother's right hand had tensed.

'It wasn't that,' Daphne replied. 'It was his conscience.'

Marion's dander was up now. 'The number of people around here who lost their sons in that war – or had them wounded – and Frank ducked out of it. What do you expect people to feel about him?'

'They could respect his point of view. He respects theirs.'

'Most folk think he was scared.'

'I've known him since school. Nothing's ever scared Frank.'

'Then, he should have fought.'

Daphne hated conversations like these. Couldn't her mother see how she felt about Frank?

She took a step back inside the room and closed the door again, the dog whining as Daphne pulled his lead. When Daphne pushed down at Pooky with her hand, he sat with a defeated look.

'You know I love Frank, don't you?' Daphne said to her mother.

'I wish you'd chuck him,' Marion said. 'You don't know how a mother feels, do you? What Robert lost, and all those others; and you're going to marry a shirker like Frank. Why does Robert have to put up with him coming around here? Have you any idea how much he hates him for ducking out of things?'

'He's told me,' Daphne said, 'but it's not Frank's fault Robert lost his arm, and I can't change what I do in my life because of it.'

Marion looked as if there was a lot more she wanted to say. 'What that war did to Robert–' she began, but Daphne did not give her the chance to finish. She turned to the dog. Pooky was no longer a duty Daphne was trying to avoid, but an opportunity. She decided to take it, gave the dog a commanding look and a pat on the head, opened the door, and allowed the dog to pull her out. A smile came to her face. Pooky still liked her. If only people were as easy to be with as dogs.

* * *

I hadn't meant to return. Leaving was such a release. Why was I back? It was a long wandering. I don't know whose boat I set off in when I left then, but it was untended, and I was glad to be able to make use of it. I rowed along the shore. I was able to follow the thrust of wind at my back as it flicked spume round me, and I leaned into the oars. The pull of arm and leg muscles, the arching of shoulder and back were soothing somehow, almost anaesthetic. All that tension in me. I had to do something with it. When I found myself at Fossmouth, I pulled the boat in among rocks. That was when I started tramping.

Casual work on farms was available and I made use of it, but it was only to get what I needed. A desperation to move onwards always pulled at me. Once I had enough money for a pack on my back, for food, cooking and eating utensils, and a sleeping roll, I had no wish to stay. I slept rough except for when I was in a shared cottage on a farm. I washed in streams. I shaved every third day to save on razors. My clothes became more and more ragged and my hair longer. I enjoyed the freedom, even revelled in the solitariness, but at no time did I ever out-tramp that anger.

At times, the image of the dead woman, her red hair catching the dying sun, would return to me; that attractive face of hers, ruined by the gash on her forehead. Underneath her body, the blood-soaked sand; beside it, the rock; and in my ears, the sound of the sea. I could barely remember striking her. And hers was not the only face that haunted me.

I found something approaching peace in the constant moving, but I never felt I escaped the thing inside me that had carried out these killings.

In time, I found company on the road. There were other tramps and I fell in with them and learned their ways. I learned to trudge from one spike to another, which was what they called the casual wards in the workhouses we moved between. When I took off my clothes, washed myself all over, and put on the workhouse garb, I felt as if I might be stepping out of one skin into another before joining the other casuals in the common dormitory, which was something I had the need to do. At least they fed you in the spikes: there was bread, dripping, water, and cheese. I didn't feel I deserved more, though I soon learned from others the art of begging and supplemented this during the day's tramp. I gave up on the casual work. I tried to become this new self – the tramp.

I remembered what it had been like when I had been with Pulteney, following on behind a young woman. He had such a fascination with a woman's voice, and I could see why. There was such lightness in it, an innocence that had never seen the things in battle that I had. I envied it, and admired it, while I hated it. It had something that I wanted for myself, and that I could never know again.

Now, I was back in Birtleby and on the path to the Ridges, and there was another young woman in front of me. This one had dark curly hair, and there was a self-righteousness in her strut that I hated. She had a dog with her, a brown-and-white spaniel cross. He was leading her a dance and did not give her any choice but to follow where he led. He took us all the way back there – where it had all happened.

As I walked behind that young woman, the rage built up inside just as it had done then. It was powerful, much stronger than I was, so irresistible I thought it must destroy me, and I wondered how I could get rid of it. We were now out in the middle of the dunes and I looked around me. There was no one else to be seen.

* * *

Pete had known these beaches boy and man. He had run about here in shorts and rushed into the sea with pals; later, he had strolled arm in arm with Marion. He knew that touch of breeze and tang of sea, and the shifting layouts of the sands; he even had names for some of these rocks. He'd always called that one turtle rock, not that it was exactly a replica of one, but naming it as that had appealed to a boy and the name had stuck; another one he knew as lion rock till Marion renamed it pussy-cat rock after studying the semi-feline outline during one stroll of theirs. Visitors to Birtleby always spent time on these beaches; in summer, there was a mass of beach huts and demurely costumed bathers. As people relaxed, they lay on deck chairs with splayed out legs and arms, often despite the rush of children's voices and limbs. Stillness, movement, peace, cheerfulness, noise: these things were what this stretch of coast signified to Pete Tanner, before the three Ridges murders. What struck Pete Tanner after those was the silence of the beaches, as visitors and locals alike shunned them. Fear – it stalked Birtleby then, and it had taken a while to be forgotten, but he felt it again now.

Pete Tanner strode forward, eyes searching one way then the other, then back again. He brushed away sweat from his brow as he drew in the long breaths that went with the pace he was setting. He had come out to look for Daphne as Pooky had returned without her. That was something that had never happened before. Where was Daphne? Why had she not come back with the dog?

When the two former soldiers, Harry Barker and Bob Nuttall, had been locked up after the first murder, it had been a relief to everyone, till the second murder was committed. It was a carbon copy of the first, and they were in prison at the time. Then a sailor, Pulteney, was charged with both killings, which was a shock, as he had been one of the main witnesses against Harry and Bob. His hanging ought to have solved everything, but then another young woman was found dead on the sands. Everybody said the police had hanged the wrong man, though this had never been proved, as the killer of the third girl was never found. Whoever that had been walked free to kill again, which fortunately he had not, and slowly people had returned to the beaches thinking the killer must have gone off elsewhere or died.

So, Daphne must be safe, must she not? And she would not have walked along towards the Ridges, would she? Especially after they had told her not to – but young folk, they never did what they were told, did they? Pete walked on with Pooky, as the dog bounded off and raced back, though Pete noticed he did not run off as far as usual. In time, Pete found himself following the animal towards the Ridges as, after all, they had been everywhere else. The dunes began to loom up before them.

Pete stared hard at the dog. Why was Pooky hanging so close to his master's heels now? Had he picked up on some of the fear that Pete was feeling among these innocent strands of marram grass and soft tumbles of sand, the spot where the murders had been done? What exactly was bothering the dog? Then, Pooky bounded off into the Ridges and Pete lost sight of him, nor could he hear any sound coming from him. Why was that?

Pete trudged over in the direction the dog had gone, his eyes sweeping everywhere. As he rounded a dune, he saw Pooky again. Pooky was pawing at something that lay in the sands, and Pete tried to work out what that was. Oh no, he thought. That was not what it looked like? But it was. Pooky was snuffling and whining at the body of a young woman. Then, Pete forced himself to walk forward. It was someone wearing a fawn jacket and skirt, just like Daphne's, and it looked like a slim young woman of about five foot six, also just like Daphne. Pete could not make out the face as a hat had been placed over it, one that Pete did not recognize, which gave him hope. Then, he remembered that Daphne had been talking about a new one she had bought. Marion had been greatly interested in this, but Pete had paid less attention. He supposed this could be it. Pete Tanner bent down to lift the hat.

CHAPTER TWO

Inspector Stephen Blades was wondering what kind of ghoulish coincidence this was, as he stood looking down at the body of another young woman in the dunes on the Ridges. His right hand reached up and tugged at his bowler hat as he sighed. He glanced across at Sergeant Peacock, took in the gloomy look on his lean face, then looked down at the body again.

This one wasn't buried, which was one difference, though there had been the usual attempt to sweep footprints away from the sand near the corpse. The familiar pool of blood lay beneath it. The hat seemed to have been placed beside the body with reverence, and that Blades had not seen before, but from what Blades had been told, it had been put there by the person who found the body. Another young woman, Blades thought, legs crooked, arms flung out, someone who had been in the flush of youth. Was there really nothing he could do to protect them? A swearword escaped his lips, acknowledged with a grunt from Peacock. Blades looked at the fashionable cut of the young woman's dress, the prettiness of the silver necklace, and the contrasting gash on the forehead. At times like these, Blades hated his job.

Blades took a note of the time as a flashbulb popped from Peacock's camera – half past four. Peacock was doing his punctilious recording of the scene.

There was a part of Blades that had been hoping the murderer who had defeated him in his first big case would return and give him another opportunity to catch him, which gave Blades a feeling of guilt. There was another young woman dead in front of him, and he might not apprehend the murderer this time either. How many more young women might die because he could not do his job? But was this the same murderer? That was yet to be established.

A movement made his head turn and he saw Parker walking towards him. The police surgeon was a neat-looking man even when called out to murder scenes such as this. Blades wondered how he succeeded in keeping his trilby so well placed on his head in the strong sea breeze. The fine cloth of his grey suit gave him the look of a man more used to fashionable circles than probing at dead bodies on a beach, and Blades doubted how well the sheen on his shoes would survive the salty sand. When Parker drew up to Blades, he put down his black leather bag as he gave Blades a smile reminiscent of a private consulting room or a fête. 'Good to see you as always, Inspector.'

'And you – if not in these circumstances.'

Parker looked down at the body and muttered. 'I could give being Police Surgeon a miss,' he said.

Blades hoped not but did not reply.

'I much prefer to meet my patients when they're still alive.' Then he paused before continuing, 'And bludgeoning someone to death like this is messy.'

He, Blades and Peacock continued to look down at the body. Then Parker reached down to his bag, opened it, extracted the required instruments, and bent towards the corpse to begin his examination. He checked first for rigor mortis, then body temperature, before studying the gash in the forehead with a glass, then the sagging, broken jaw.

'Not much doubt about cause of death, and there's been more than one blow, though the first one probably killed her. All the second one would have done was break the jaw, and I wonder at the need for it. I suppose in the fever of the moment he had to make sure. He was determined to kill her, so, not manslaughter.' He paused, then looked around him. 'The weapon was probably a rock.'

'No. We don't see it anywhere around either,' Blades said. 'Can you state the time of death?'

'With the normal level of accuracy.' Then, Parker paused as he gave thought to his reply. 'Though this one isn't difficult. A couple of hours ago, no later, though possibly not as long ago as that.'

Blades was pleased. Parker was giving reasonable precision to his estimate. 'One and a half to two hours ago?' Blades said.

Parker opened his mouth as if to speak, then closed it again.

'That's what you said, isn't it?' Blades asked.

'Yes, and, as you'll have noticed yourself–'

'Noticed what?'

'This is not unlike the work of our previous friend.'

'Very like.'

'Indeed.'

'Can you say with certainty that it was?'

'Not absolutely.'

'So, it could be a copycat. The details of those murders were well publicised.'

'True.'

'They could have been imitated by anybody,' Peacock said.

'Not that there was much to copy,' Parker said. 'A hit over the head somewhere on the Ridges.'

'Easy enough,' Peacock agreed.

'Or the murderer could have returned,' Parker said. 'Thinking of the pathology of the previous murders, I didn't think he would stop at all.'

'Which he did,' Peacock said.

'Apparently,' Blades said.

'Until his return,' Parker said. 'Of course, our study of the psychology of mass murderers is limited. We hang them.'

'As we should,' Blades said.

'True,' Parker replied. 'Though sometimes I think it a pity we don't delay it a bit in the interests of science.'

'You won't find any of the relatives of victims will agree with you,' Blades said.

'Probably,' Parker said. 'To tell the truth, I was hoping this mass murderer had just died. There was that murderer they caught and executed in the USA,' Parker said. 'There was speculation he'd done our Ridges murders as well, even though he denied it.'

Reports had emerged in the press of a murderer in California who had committed a not dissimilar act over there and, oddly enough, he had been British and living in Leeds at the time of the Ridges murders. He had only moved to the USA after they had stopped.

'It can't be him,' Blades said. 'No one can come back from the dead.'

'It's a copycat or the same murderer, and, whichever it is, we'll catch him this time, sir,' Peacock said.

'Definitely,' Blades agreed as he shot Peacock a grateful look. He had suffered over those Ridges murders, and it was typical of Peacock to notice his sensitivities. Blades felt himself tense as he thought of his boss, Chief Constable Moffat, and wondered what his reaction would be to this. Moffat had been shaken by the publicity attached to the Ridges murders and the questions that had been asked. The public reaction had been that they'd hanged an innocent man. Blades remembered the pressure they had all been under then and he was aware that it could return with this murder. He thought of what his wife Jean had to suffer, and he regretted what she might have to go through now. It was the public criticism of Blades she had found excruciating, not that Blades had even been the senior officer responsible for the cases. Walker from the Yard had been brought in over that one, and he had been dismissed because of the perceived failures in his investigation, though not even that had deflected all the criticism from Blades. Jean had put pressure on her husband to leave the force, and Blades could have been tempted by this, had he not felt so much for these young victims. Now he seemed to be going through it all again.

'I'll arrange for an ambulance to take the body to the mortuary,' Parker said.

Blades did not reply but continued staring at the body.

'We'll have the PM arranged as soon as possible,' Parker continued.

Now Blades looked up at him. 'Thanks,' he said.

Blades and Peacock remained at the murder scene after Parker had departed, their eyes probing everywhere. Blades frowned. 'This area needs a thorough search. That murder weapon's probably around somewhere.'

'It must be,' Peacock said. 'Who would take a rock away with them?'

'Assuming it was a rock. Arrange for constables to do a trawl of the whole area for anything suitable. It will have blood on it. That will tell them when they've found it. And I need to arrange for a report in the newspapers and an appeal for witnesses. Someone must have seen him around here.'

'Assuming they realised what they were looking at.'

'They'll know when they read that newspaper report,' Blades replied.

'Which theory are you going to follow, sir? Copycat or the same murderer?'

'We can't assume anything. We have to uncover facts and follow them up.'

'Of course, sir.'

'We'll need to also review prior cases, of course, look at previous suspects and any possible follow-ups to statements and leads that didn't look promising then, but could now.'

'I wasn't convinced about the direction of the investigations then, sir.'

Blades looked at him with surprise.

'I didn't go with the press theory that they were all murdered by the same man. The last one, the one that was done after Pulteney's hanging, could have been a copycat,' Peacock said.

'A bit of an odd one with someone already hanged for the first two murders.'

Peacock ignored Blades' penetrating stare.

'And three young women alone on the same stretch of beach in similar circumstances with no witnesses in sight,' Peacock said. 'Just how likely is that? You wouldn't think any young woman would have gone near there by herself after the first one, never mind the second.'

Blades gave this thought before replying. 'That was said at the time, but that's what appeared to happen.'

'I don't believe it. They went along there with someone. Who else did the young women know? Did Daphne know any of the same people as Elspeth Summers, the last Ridges victim?'

'Which we will cover. If there's an overlap with relationships, we'll find it.'

'And, for the record, I think the likeliest thing is the sailor Pulteney did the first two Ridges murders. We know he was there. He pretended to be a witness to one of them. It's never been proved you didn't get the right man. There were too many knee-jerk reactions going on then, particularly from administrators without personal stakes looking after their own jobs.'

'Moffat?'

Peacock did not answer that question. 'I do think the third one was a copycat, possibly the same murderer as this one.'

'Interesting,' Blades said.

'I wondered about Chris Fleming. He was a witness to both the first murder and the second.'

'So did we. We couldn't place him anywhere near the third murder. And we probably won't be able to find him now. He left the area and hasn't been heard of since.'

'It would be interesting if we found out he's come back.'

Blades gave this thought. 'Wouldn't it? Still, we're nowhere near theories on this murder yet. We haven't even finished examining the murder scene.'

'At least we don't have to do any work to find out who the victim is.'

'That's true. We can examine all her movements over the last week or so and all her relationships. And our first inquiries will be along the lines that she could have been murdered by someone who knew her. Then we can see if there are any links with anything else previous. And, as I say, we haven't finished examining this murder scene.'

Blades stood and looked at the scene. As Peacock started taking more photographs, Blades spoke to him again.

'You think we were right with Pulteney after all?'

'I'm sure of it, sir.'

CHAPTER THREE

The Tanners' apartment was in one of the older sandstone buildings in Birtleby. Blades noted the weathering on the stone as he and Peacock approached, before he took in the flaking paint on the windows. As he looked up at the slate roof, he noticed repairs that needed doing. He wondered what he would encounter inside the flat.

Marion Tanner herself welcomed them at the front door and ushered them into a small and barely furnished room that doubled as kitchen and sitting room, but which was, Blades noted, clean; the paint and the brown-patterned wallpaper on the walls were newish and smart. Pete Tanner was seated in front of the fire, ramming tobacco into a pipe. There was a grim look to his face as he looked up at them. Blades felt awkward and threatening as he stood above him looking down. The momentary silence was broken by Marion offering them seats. It felt marginally more natural when they were all seated and on the same level. On the fireplace, Blades noticed a framed photograph of a young woman, whom he took to be Daphne. There were also photographs of Pete and Marion Tanner and a young man in uniform. Blades was wondering how to begin his questioning, when Pete spoke.

'Have you discovered anything yet?'

Blades tried to take in exactly what that attitude was. There was an authority in the voice, but Blades' strongest impression was of anxiety mixed with something else, and, yes, that would be anger. He supposed Pete Tanner had the right to it.

Blades adopted a calm tone of voice. 'It takes time. We're following our procedures, and one of the first things we need to do is seek information from the relatives of the victim.'

Marion leaned forward to speak and Blades noted the sincerity in her voice. 'We'll do everything we can to help,' she said.

'Definitely,' Pete said. Some of the tension seemed to have left his face, now replaced by dutiful concern. 'Fire away.'

'Do you know why Daphne was on the beach?' Blades asked.

'She was walking the dog,' Marion replied. 'It's Robert's job but he hadn't done it, and I can never get Pete to exercise Pooky. He's a postman, and he always says trudging round Birtleby is exercise enough for him. But we did tell her to go nowhere near the Ridges.'

'So, you don't know why she was there?'

'No.'

'Who's Robert?' Blades asked.

'Her brother,' Pete explained.

'Does he live here as well?'

'Yes,' Marion replied.

'And what does he work at?' Blades asked.

There was an embarrassed look on Pete's face as he answered. 'Nothing at the moment. He was a tailor, but he hasn't settled down to a job again since he came back from the war.'

'They can be difficult to get,' Blades said.

'That's true,' Pete said, 'particularly when you've lost an arm. There's no way he can go back to what he did after that.'

'I suppose not,' Blades said, 'it was a terrible thing that war, disrupted a lot of lives.'

'You're telling me,' Pete said.

'Do you know where he was when Daphne was out with your dog?'

'The simple answer is no,' Marion replied. 'He was supposed to be the one taking the dog out, but he was nowhere to be seen. Probably over at Helen's. Helen is his girlfriend.'

'So, where would we find her?'

'Helen lives with her parents on Church Street,' Pete said. 'Robert might be there. He's out and about somewhere.'

'Do you have a number?'

'15.'

'Thank you. Did Daphne have a boyfriend?'

'Yes,' Marion replied. 'Frank Bywaters.'

Blades tried to work out her feelings about him as she said this.

'She's known him for years. He's the son of a local schoolteacher.'

'Bit of a catch then?' Blades asked.

A look of disgust appeared on Marion's face, which puzzled Blades, followed by a look of defensiveness on Pete's.

'Marion was always taken with Frank before the war. There's a fineness about him – but he came out to be a conscientious objector.'

'That would have been controversial,' Blades said.

'Particularly when everyone else's son has gone off to war,' Marion said.

Now they both stopped speaking, as if heavy thoughts were occupying them. What Blades was thinking was that Frank sounded an unlikely suspect if he was a CO, though plenty of doubts had been expressed as to their genuineness by some. As far as Blades could see, the problem with conscientious objectors was that they did mean what they said.

'Could she have gone to see him?' he asked.

'All we know is she left here with the dog, and then the dog came back by itself,' Marion said.

'Do you have Frank's address?' Blades asked.

Pete told him it.

Blades spoke to Pete. 'When you went down to the Ridges, did you see anyone else there going to or coming away from the place?'

Pete gave this some thought.

'There was a couple,' he said.

'Did you know them, or could you describe them?'

'Young. He was tall. She was slight. She didn't look like any more than a schoolgirl.'

'Would you know them again?'

'I think so.'

'Do you know of anyone Daphne crossed lately, or who has been showing unusual interest in her?'

Neither Pete nor Marion could help with that.

Blades thought it was probably time to leave as there was nothing to be gained from upsetting the parents of the murder victim further. 'If you come down to the station when you can, we'll have your statements taken, and we'll want a detailed description of that couple you saw. Oh, and would you ask Robert to come down as well? We need to talk to everyone in Daphne's family.'

* * *

There was a troubled silence for some time after Blades and Peacock had left. Pete found himself unable to meet Marion's eyes at all and busied himself by picking up his pipe again and trying to light it. He sensed that Marion at no time stopped looking in his direction. Then Marion spoke.

'Daphne did nothing to deserve being killed.'

'I know,' Pete replied. He continued his performance with the pipe as Marion continued to watch him.

'Couldn't you have taken the dog out just that once?' she said.

Pete did not reply. He puffed at the tobacco and took satisfaction in the beginning of a glow. Then, he looked up at Marion, whose eyes were still boring in his direction.

'You're right,' he said. 'I wish I had.'

'I'm sorry,' she said. 'You're not to blame.'

To Pete, the words sounded empty, said for the sake of it, but he could not blame her for feeling as she did. 'I feel as if I am,' he replied, 'but I don't know what to do about it.' His voice was breaking with hurt, but he did his best to keep a manly expression on his face. 'If I could undo it, I would.'

Tears overwhelmed Marion, and Pete laid down the pipe and put his arms around her. When her weeping had subsided, Marion repeated, 'It's not your fault.' Pete was at a loss for words. What words of comfort could cover any of this? He continued to struggle with his emotions, then had to admit defeat. Tears gushed out of him, as he could do nothing but say, 'I'm sorry' over and over again. Then Marion's chest began to heave, and they were both in sobs together with their arms round each other. After the sobs had died out, they did not move or speak. What was there to be said or done?

Then the door opened, and Robert walked in. There was an odd, angry expression on his face and Pete thought he must have heard the news already, but Robert stopped and drew himself up at the sight of them, now giving a look of incomprehension. 'It's your sister,' Pete said. 'Something dreadful has happened.'

Robert stared back. Then Marion spoke. 'Daphne's been murdered. She's dead.'

'You can't mean it?' Robert said.

'I found her body myself,' Pete said. 'Down at the Ridges. She was out walking Pooky but Pooky came back by himself. So, I went out to look for her.' Then the words stopped, and Pete could only stare ahead of him.

'What was she doing at the Ridges?' Robert asked.

'I know. Precisely where she would never go, where she was told never to go anyway.'

'What are the police doing?'

'Investigating?' Pete said. It had been upsetting trying to comfort a disintegrating wife, and now he was looking at his son and Pete did not think he had ever seen Robert's face look quite like that. 'They've been questioning us, and now they say they want to question you.'

A flash of anger appeared on Robert's face. 'And we don't know anything,' Robert said, 'so that won't help much.'

'No,' Pete agreed.

'And they say they want to question Frank,' Marion said.

'I suppose they would,' Robert said.

'Where were you?' Marion asked.

Pete noticed that Robert paused before answering, then said quickly, 'With Helen.' Guilt was all over Robert's face. 'I suppose,' he said, 'it should have been me out with that dog.'

But Marion's first reaction to her son was supportive. 'You mustn't think like that,' she said. 'Who could have predicted anything like this?'

Robert's eyes glazed for a moment. Then he said, 'I still can't believe this.'

'We don't want to,' Pete said.

'No,' Marion agreed.

'She was so full of life,' Robert said.

'So full of being with Frank too,' Marion said. 'She had so much to look forward to, she said.'

'She doted on him,' Robert said.

Pete noticed the look of irritation on Robert's face as he said that, hardly surprising, knowing Robert's feelings about Frank, but he noticed that Robert tried to dismiss the reaction.

'It's that Ridges murderer,' Robert said. 'He's come back. Who else could it be?'

'They should have caught him the last time,' Marion said. 'I hope they do this time.'

'If they know what they're doing,' Robert said, 'which they don't seem to.'

'It was that Inspector Blades who was leading the questions,' Pete said.

'He should have been sacked over the Ridges murders at the time,' Robert said. 'How many more girls have to be murdered before they start taking this seriously? I could lynch him, never mind the Ridges murderer.'

Pete could agree with that, so what was puzzling him about Robert? He had behaved exactly as might have been expected and said all the right things, but there was something. That was it. If Daphne's death was news to Robert, what was the explanation for that odd mood he was already in when he came back?

CHAPTER FOUR

HAS THE RIDGES MURDERER
RETURNED?

A horrific find has been made at Birtleby on the very same stretch of beach where the Ridges Murders occurred. Once again, the body of a young woman has been discovered, a twenty-two-year-old unmarried woman from Birtleby called Daphne Tanner. She was exercising the family dog on the beach when the tragedy occurred. The body was discovered at half-past three in the afternoon and it is thought that the murder would have occurred from half-an-hour to an hour before. Death was by a blow to the head. The police investigation is led by Inspector Blades, the officer who apprehended the murderer in the Wright case. The police are asking for any potential witnesses to step forward. In particular, the police would be interested in speaking with anyone who saw Daphne in the company of another person or persons that afternoon. Daphne is described as slim, attractive and having dark curly hair. She was five foot six and dressed in a fawn jacket and skirt. She wore a fawn cloche hat.

The dog is described as being of the liver-and-white spaniel type. If anyone has seen anything suspicious on or near the beach, they are asked to please come forward to Birtleby Police Station.

When the newspaper containing this article landed on his desk, Blades was writing up his initial report, while, across from him, Peacock was studying his photographs of the murder site. Blades picked the paper up and perused the article. He frowned, re-read it, then threw it in Peacock's direction. Blades watched as Peacock turned his attention to it. Peacock looked back up at him.

'It seems to cover it, sir.'

'Should we have released more information, do you think?' Blades replied.

'We haven't much more to give yet,' Peacock said. 'This could produce results. Someone must have seen her that afternoon. She wasn't invisible and neither is anyone else.'

'Wouldn't it be good if someone turned up who'd witnessed the actual murder this time?'

'When does that ever happen?'

'Not often. We still don't know why she went out to the Ridges. There are more accessible places to exercise a dog.'

'In other words, who was the person she was with?' Peacock had swivelled his chair round so that he was facing Blades.

'Her boyfriend Frank Bywaters springs to mind,' Blades replied. 'Courting couples do go out there. I wonder if he has an alibi. I suppose anyone can lose their temper and lash out, even conscientious objectors.'

Peacock's brows were pursed together as he leaned back in his chair. 'Sounds a bit unbelievable for a CO, but I suppose he could have been damaged in the war, CO or not. He didn't do any fighting, but some COs were in France with the Non-Combatant Corps, and not far behind the lines if not in them. They could have got shellshock as easily as anyone else – and they were treated like shirkers. Conchies were about as unpopular as the Germans. That kind of thing can wear a man down.'

Blades nodded. 'Daphne's brother Robert was worn down,' he said.

'More than a bit. He lost an arm.'

'And his job.'

Blades stood up and strode for a couple of steps, then turned toward Peacock. 'But why kill his sister? We need to know more about that relationship. And we don't know what his movements were yet.'

'If it is the Ridges murderer again,' Peacock said, 'Daphne might not even have known the man who killed her.'

Blades looked at Peacock. He took in the intentness in his eyes. It was reassuring to have a sergeant as passionate about cases as himself. They might somehow get to the end of them. 'It doesn't quite fit the pattern of the Ridges murderer. The body wasn't buried, and the murder weapon was moved so far away this time. It's surprising those Police Constables found it. I suppose he did the deed and carried off the rock without realising it was in his hand, then, when he did, he chucked it. Not quite the way the Ridges murderer behaved.'

'A copycat not copied as closely as intended would be one thought.'

A good insight, Blades thought, which he was grateful for. But Blades himself did not feel clever, just desperate as always at the beginning of cases.

'We have a few avenues to explore,' Blades said. 'We need a few answers too.'

'I still think she must have gone there with someone. Her father said they'd told Daphne not to go to the Ridges. She knew about them. So why else would she go there?'

'Did she have other friends? Who did she know?' Blades asked. 'She worked at a milliner's. Did she know someone from there? She must have done.'

The men sat in silence for a moment. Peacock leafed through his photographs. 'I did find something interesting,' he said. He picked up one photograph and showed it to Blades. 'Bring it closer,' Blades said.

The sand had been soft in lots of places, so Blades had seen no distinct footprints on the site, but that photograph did seem to have shown up something, not quite a clear footprint but a suggestion of one, and Blades studied it. 'A man's,' he said. 'Somewhere between an 8 and a 10. No precise tread.'

'Look beside the footprint. Half buried in the sand.'

'A cigarette stub. That must have been picked up.'

'No. It wasn't.'

'They missed it?'

'They must have done.'

'An Abdullah perhaps? Didn't that figure in the first murder?'

'Lots of people smoke those.'

'Not that many. They're expensive.'

'I wonder if it's still there. I'll go and check on that.'

'Do,' Blades said. 'Though we're probably clutching at straws. No. Correct that. Cigarette ends.' Blades laughed. 'Well spotted, though. And there might be something else we've missed in those photographs. Leave those with me. We need every fact we can get. We haven't nearly enough of those yet. We could do with witnesses coming forward. And we need to question Frank Bywaters and Robert Tanner.'

Then Blades sat back in his seat again and frowned. There were nothing but half-grasped facts at the moment, and his mind always raced like this when he didn't know nearly enough. But the chase had begun. The challenge had been laid down, and he and Peacock were in the midst of their response.

* * *

The witness was an elderly woman with a vague air. She was stout or had been. Her body was large in frame, but her skin sagged as if weight had been sucked out of it. She looked around at the witness room in Birtleby Police Station as if having difficulty taking in her surroundings, then blinked as her glance settled on Blades. She giggled to herself almost like a schoolgirl, then asked to sit down after already heaving herself into one of the chairs in front of Blades' and Peacock's desk. Sergeant Ryan had seen her when she arrived and ushered her through. Looking at her, Blades wondered if she should have been ushered away. But he settled to his task.

'You have some information for us in connection to the body found in the sands?'

The lady had a large gnarled stick which she leaned on even when she was seated. Her breath wheezed. She said nothing at first, seeming to be having difficulty in gathering her breath well enough to speak. The effort of reaching the station had perhaps taken a lot out of her.

'Your name is?' Peacock asked.

'Mrs Randall,' she said, with a rasp in her voice. Then she drew in a deep breath and spoke again. 'Mrs Alice Randall. I live on the seafront and often spend time sitting on one of the benches there. It's relaxing looking out over the beach and out to sea, and I know a lot of people here, and they often stop to speak. And the air is fresh, and it clears the lungs.'

'Of course,' Blades said. He nodded and waited for whatever it was Mrs Randall had made such an effort to gather herself to say.

'He was a genuine tramp.'

'He was?'

'Oh yes. He hadn't shaved in a while and those clothes were ragged, and how he managed to get about in those battered boots I dread to think.'

'Had you seen him before?' Peacock asked.

'Oh no. I've never come across him before in my life. At least I don't think so. One tramp can look a bit like another, I suppose, and there are so many old soldiers on the road these days. That war was dreadful. I hate seeing soldiers with medals begging or selling bootlaces, don't you? I've felt sorry for them before and offered to buy the whole tray, but they don't like that. Now, why wouldn't they? I'd happily pay over the odds for it and you'd think it would save them a bit of effort and give them a bit of money. But no. They don't mind how much over the odds you're prepared to pay for one pair of laces, but they hold onto that tray like grim death. I suppose they make more money like that. I don't know. They can be a bit rude though, which is a bit much when you're only trying to be helpful.'

Blades wondered where she was going with this. He started tapping a finger, noticed that he was doing this, then stopped himself. Peacock was keeping up a good display of polite interest. Perhaps he, Blades, ought to try harder.

'So, he was behaving oddly that afternoon?'

'Oh yes. Very.'

She paused as if to gather her thoughts but, as this only resulted in a particularly long pause, Blades spoke again. 'In what way?'

'Let's see. He was following her, you know.'

'Following who?'

'The girl who was found dead on the beach.'

Mrs Randall now had Blades' and Peacock's full attention.

'How do you know it was her?'

'Because I read the description in the paper and because I know her. I've often shopped in that milliner's she worked in. Daphne Tanner. A bit slow with her service, I thought. I don't think she was all that bright. But she was pleasant enough. A pretty smile, I thought. It often occurred to me she must be popular with the boys.

But I wouldn't know. I didn't really know her as such. I've no idea what she got up to.'

'But you saw her that afternoon?'

'Oh yes. With that silly dog of hers. And a bit of a mind of its own it has. I've seen it sit on the ground and refuse to walk any further with her. Then change its mind when she agreed to go in the direction it wanted to go in. Pooky. That was the name. You often heard her calling out to it. "Pooky. Pooky. Come here at once." And the dog just keeping on running wherever it wanted to. The Ridges. That was where the dog was determined to go that day. And that man following her. I nearly called out to her. I wish I had now. But people object if you interfere in their business, and you don't like to.'

'Can you describe the man?' Blades asked.

'He was a tramp.'

'And?' Blades said.

'He looked like any other tramp. Down at heel. Battered, old slouch hat on his head. Shifty look. Mean eyes. Not very good teeth.'

'Could you say how tall he was?'

'The stoop he had on that back of his, I don't know. Sort of average height?'

'Anything distinctive about his face?'

'His face? A bit mean, I suppose. But like any tramp's face, and they all look much the same to me. Self-pitying and short-tempered. You could feel more sympathy for them if they were a bit better natured. But I suppose if they have to tramp about all the time, that would make them a bit miserable.'

'So, this tramp was short-tempered about something? What did he do to make you think that?'

'Do? Oh. Nothing. But tramps tend to be like that. The ones I meet always are.'

The way she rambled on, Blades thought he could see why, but made sure that didn't show on his face. 'Can you be precise in any way about what he looked like?'

Mrs Randall thought for a few moments.

'I suppose,' she started to say, then stopped. 'He looked just like any tramp going about. Sort of shuffled a bit like they do, as if his feet were a bit sore.'

'Did he speak at all to you or the girl?'

'He didn't say anything, just followed on after her.'

'Did you see how far he followed her?'

'It's quite a long way from the Ridges where I sit.'

'Where is that?'

'Just in front of the big white house.'

'Ridgeway House?'

'That's the one.'

'That is a bit of a distance from there. So, you don't know if he was just going in the same direction as the girl or whether he did follow her as such right into the Ridges?'

'I suppose,' Mrs Randall said. A deflated look came over her face.

Blades smiled patiently in reply. 'But thank you for coming forward with the information. It could be extremely useful. We don't know at this stage. My sergeant will take your statement.' He rang the bell for Sergeant Ryan and, after Mrs Randall had been led out, spoke to Peacock. 'What do you think?'

'She definitely recognized Daphne Tanner. And she has reported an average looking tramp with nothing to distinguish him from any other one and who could have been following her or not. Does that sum it up?'

'Succinct, Sergeant Peacock. Yes, it does.'

'All the same,' Peacock said, 'it sounds interesting.'

'Yes, it does.'

'There are a lot of ex-soldiers amongst tramps. And they were all trained to kill.'

CHAPTER FIVE

When Robert and his father turned up at the station, Blades and Peacock had been about to leave to follow up on a report, but Blades delayed that. The pair were now seated opposite them in the interview room.

Robert's eyes moved around the room, then moved around it again, though, as the interview room was deliberately bare, there was not much to take in. Pete Tanner let his eyes settle somewhere above Blades and to his right.

Blades adopted a benign tone. 'So, you're Robert Tanner?' he said.

'That's why I'm here,' Robert said. His voice was cutting.

Robert was a thin man with a pinched face and a self-righteous set to the jaw. Blades could not help but notice the empty sleeve on Robert's right side and the clench of the fist on the one arm he did possess.

'Would you tell us where you were on Tuesday afternoon?'

'I could. Can you tell me why you're sitting in your comfortable police station instead of being out catching Daphne's murderer?'

This young man was worked up, Blades thought. Pete had given a quick intake of breath, muttered, 'Robert', and glanced away as if wishing he was somewhere else. Blades tried to work out how to respond to Robert; aware of the tightening in his lips, Blades did his best to keep his face neutral, but the note of authority in his voice was deliberate.

'So, would you outline your movements to us, sir?'

'I suppose,' Robert replied. He seemed a bit disappointed at not receiving more of a reaction from Blades. He glared at Peacock, whose expression remained inscrutable as he sat with his pencil raised above his notebook. 'Not that it will help you,' Robert said. 'I wasn't anywhere near the Ridges.'

'So, you were where, sir?'

'I was with Helen. She's the girl I go about with.'

'And where was this?'

'At her parents' house. It's on Church Street. That's at the other end of town – as I expect you know.'

'So it is, sir. When did you arrive there and when did you leave?'

Robert gave him another glower, but answered, 'I must have got there about one and left about half two.'

'And what did you do after that?'

'I went for a bit of a walk, but nowhere near the Ridges.' Robert paused and sighed. 'I'll tell you what it was. Helen had just told me she'd finished with me.'

Pete looked across at Robert with surprise. 'What?'

Robert turned to him. 'It surprised me too. But she's taken the notion into her head.' Emotion took over his face and he struggled to control it. 'She's got someone with two arms.'

'That's what she said?' his father asked.

'No. But that's what it will be.'

'Did she say she had somebody else?'

'She'll be protecting him from me by her way of things, but I'll find out soon enough.'

Peacock stopped his writing and looked at Robert with what Blades could see was now sympathy. Blades was trying to work out exactly what Robert was like beneath that petulant behaviour. There was bitterness there. How deep was it and what could it lead to? 'Protecting him from you, sir?' he asked.

Robert gave Blades a look of contempt. He reached his hand over to his empty sleeve and flapped it at Blades. 'I might say something unpleasant to him, I suppose. I'm not going to do anything else.'

As intended, Blades could not avoid a feeling of guilt about the question, yet it had been valid; and he had noticed something else in that anger of Robert's. Yes. That was arrogance.

'And I went for a long walk after that, to relieve my feelings. Which is why I didn't go straight home.'

'I see, sir.'

'I was devastated. Helen stuck by me all through the war. Even after I lost my arm. And now this. It's hard to take.'

Blades respected Robert's right to his feelings, but that would not stop the questions. 'So, where did you go if you didn't go straight back to your parents' house?'

'Along the shore. But nowhere near the Ridges.' Blades noted the repetition. 'I went the opposite way,' Robert added.

'Did anyone see you?' Blades asked.

'I expect someone did, but I can't say that I was paying attention. I could have walked past the King without noticing. I was lost in my thoughts, a bit bitter, I suppose.'

'It would be understandable.'

'Do we need to go over this? I don't see how this helps you.'

Blades ignored that, and asked, 'What time did you arrive home?'

Pete was looking at Blades with an anxiety that was turning to anger. He spoke with emphasis. 'At about six, which was the first he knew anything about the murder. I can vouch for that.'

Blades continued to study Robert. 'Do you know anyone your sister might have had a quarrel with?'

'She wasn't the sort to have arguments with people, though I suppose someone might have been having a go at her about Frank.'

'That's her boyfriend?'

'Her fiancé.'

'Because he was a conscientious objector?'

'That's right.'

'Was there anyone in particular who'd been doing that?'

Robert thought for a moment. 'I can't think of anyone annoyed enough to kill her.'

'Did anyone have a romantic interest in her, apart from Frank Bywaters?'

'She wouldn't have encouraged anyone. She was struck with Frank.'

'And she didn't complain about anyone bothering her?'

'No.'

'Usually the killer is someone who knows the victim. If you can think of anyone else she was close to, we would be grateful for the information.'

But Robert's anger was mounting. 'You know who did it. The homicidal maniac is back. The one you should have caught before. If you'd done your job better then, Daphne would be alive today.'

Blades said nothing, though he did resent the tone. If Robert knew what he had gone through over those previous murders, he might think better of him than that.

Then he spoke. 'Homicidal maniac is one theory, sir. We haven't finished gathering enough facts yet to be sure about anything.'

Robert now pointed at Blades with the index finger of his one hand. 'Well, be sure about this. I've answered your questions and I doubt if any of them were helpful to you.

It's time you started doing something useful and left innocent people alone.'

'Now, Robert,' his father said, his eyes intent but with that patience back. He turned to Blades. 'I apologise for him. He's upset. He's had a particularly difficult time.'

'I appreciate that, sir.' But the look Blades gave Robert was not apologetic. 'You appreciate that we might have to ask you further questions in the course of our investigations?'

Robert opened his mouth as if to say something, but his father's gaze stopped him. Pete spoke for Robert. 'We do, Inspector. Thank you for your restraint.'

As his father led him from the room, what sounded like a snort of anger exploded from Robert.

* * *

The broad bay windows and the stained-glass, mahogany front door were the first things that Blades noticed about the Bywaters' house, as he and Sergeant Peacock strode up the path leading to it. Unlike the Tanners' place, this was no humble post-office worker's apartment, but a middle-class home situated behind a well-cultivated garden in a leafy street.

'No wonder Daphne's keen on him,' Peacock muttered.

'If the boyfriend is as impressive as the boyfriend's house, yes,' Blades replied.

Blades pressed the doorbell. A servant answered, Blades handed over his card, and waited for her return. When she did, she ushered them into a high-ceilinged hall with a wooden settle and an ornate stand holding a giant aspidistra. The young woman took their jackets and hats, and hung them on a mirrored oak hallstand, then led them into a sitting room where the master and lady of the house were seated.

Blades adopted his most charming smile. 'Good evening. Mr and Mrs Bywaters?'

Though seated, the man gave the impression of some height. He was thin and ascetic looking and wore a pince-nez, which he took off and laid on the table beside the book he had been reading. 'Alan Bywaters. And this is May, my wife,' he said, gesturing to the woman beside him.

'Pleased to meet you,' Blades said.

'How can we help?'

'It's your son we're here to see. Is he around?'

'You've come about the death of Daphne?'

Blades gave him a careful look. 'That's correct.'

'We thought you'd be over. He has visited her parents to give his condolences. They're bereft – as he is. It was a shock. But they took so long in getting around to telling Frank. We heard from the neighbourhood shop before we heard from them.'

'They ought to have given him more consideration than that,' May said. May was an elegant looking woman, in a high-necked dress. Her carefully-tended hair was long but swept up on top of her head. The brooch that sparkled from her front held green stones that Blades took to be emeralds.

'They've had a lot to take in,' Blades said. 'It's a difficult thing to adjust to.'

'May we ask how she died?' May asked.

'A blow to the head,' Blades replied. 'Death would have been instantaneous.'

'I suppose that's something,' May said.

'It wasn't a lengthy ordeal for her,' Blades said.

'Not that anything is a consolation for the loss of a life,' Alan said. 'But still, she wasn't… she wasn't…'

'Interfered with in any way? No,' Blades said.

'Thank God for that,' May said.

'You were very fond of her?' Blades asked.

A strange expression came over May's face and she took time over her reply. 'She seemed nice enough. Frank was very keen on her.'

'May wanted someone better than her for Frank. She wasn't from our class. But she was a likeable girl,' Alan said.

'Frank liked her and when Frank makes his mind up about something, nothing changes it.' There was a hint of bitterness in the lines round May's mouth as she said this.

Alan's eyes took on a hint of irritation but also some pride. 'He's a socialist to the core, our Frank. Has been since university. Class makes no difference to him. And she was a respectable girl.'

'He's always been too stubborn,' May said.

'It shows character,' Alan said. 'I admired him for his stance in the war. Not that I agreed with it. His brother was an officer. We are a patriotic family. And we'd never heard of such a thing as conscientious objectors. At least he was prepared to work in the Non-Combatant Corps.'

'Despite the arguments Clifford put forward to him,' May said.

'I told him not to listen to those. Clifford's a born martyr. That's his trouble.'

'Clifford Allen?' Blades said.

'That's right, one of the leaders of the Conscientious Objectors' movement.'

'I've heard of him too, sir,' Peacock said. 'Frank wasn't what they termed an absolutist, then?'

'Frank was prepared to accept orders and wear a uniform, unlike Clifford and some of the rest; and he would contribute to the war effort even if he wouldn't kill anybody. And I agreed with that.'

'So, he wasn't one of those sent to prison?'

'Or put on those work details. You should have seen Clifford after the war. He'd lost two stone and he was thin to begin with.'

'Just being in the Non-Combatant Corps made Frank unpopular, as you can imagine,' May said. 'And it didn't make him more eligible as a bachelor.'

'So, he might have thought it just as well to settle on Daphne as she was keen?' Blades asked.

A frown came over May's face and she opened her mouth to reply, but at that moment a young man strode into the room. Blades scrutinised him, considering whether he might be their murderer. He had his father's build and height, and, like him, possessed an intelligent-looking face, high cheekbones, and a prominent nose and ears. Blades noted it was a strong face with a firm jaw and a questioning look in the eyes.

'Ah,' Frank said when he saw Blades and Peacock. He stopped in mid-stride.

His father spoke. 'Inspector Blades and Sergeant Peacock. They're here about Daphne.'

'I expect they are,' Frank said.

'I'm sorry for your loss,' Blades said.

Frank looked unsure how to respond, then said, 'Thank you. It's been a shock.' Then, a strong emotion surged through him. He turned away, walked over to a seat and sat in it before looking in Blades' direction again. His face was white, the lips taut.

Blades repeated what he had told Frank's parents about Daphne's death. 'Do you know of any enemies she may have had, sir?'

Frank's stare at Blades was grim, and Blades wondered if he would be able to answer, but he did. 'She was a particularly inoffensive person. I'm not. I've upset everybody in Birtleby, I think. I hope nobody took that out on her.'

'You were a conscientious objector?'

'Guilty as charged.'

'You did your bit in the war, sir. You were in the Non-Combatant Corps.'

'Thank you. Even though I am a socialist,' Frank pointed out. 'And we were even out in France.'

'There are a lot of socialists around, sir.' And it didn't stop them fighting was the thought in Blades' head. He frowned and tried to work Frank out.

'I'm an international socialist,' Frank said. 'It was always my opinion that the Great War was perpetrated by capitalists who duped the working class into fighting so they could profit from the conflict.'

Some weariness came over Blades at that remark. Jean had lost her brother on the Front and he thought of the pain she still carried because of that.

'If the international brotherhood of workers had refused to fight, there would have been no war,' Frank said, and there was the look of the preacher on his face.

Blades forced patience into his voice. 'You may be right, sir.' But what came into his mind as he said it was a picture of Jean crying herself to sleep after the telegram arrived. This man said there was no point to the war her brother had died in? Oh yes. That sort of comment could gain a response.

'Did you get hostile reactions from anyone in Birtley?'

Frank laughed. 'I'm sure half the town's against me, but it'll settle down. The war's over. And they're good people around here really.'

'No one has been violent to you?'

'No.'

Blades looked at Frank but saw no reason to doubt what he had said.

'And can you tell me about your own movements on Tuesday afternoon?'

'You want to know where I was?' A look of annoyance swept over Frank's face, but he controlled it. 'Let's see. I do teach, but it's only part-time. It's all I can get at the moment. I couldn't get my job back after the war. The parents at my school wouldn't have me back and it was difficult finding any other school that would take me. As you might expect, I suppose. Schools were nothing but honest when they interviewed me. Their priority was to provide jobs for men who were returning from fighting in the war, and they looked at me as if I'd just crawled out from under a stone before showing me the door. I think that was the only reason I got some interviews – so they could have the satisfaction of doing that. But I've got somewhere part-time now. So, yes. That day, I was working in the morning but not the afternoon, so I could have murdered Daphne, if that's what you mean.'

Blades did not turn down the chance of a direct question. 'Did you?'

'Did I hell,' he said. 'Go and bother someone else, why don't you?' Then Frank found restraint and pursed his lips.

Blades did not reply to Frank's remark. He studied the expression on Frank's face instead. He decided to continue with more unsettling questions, though they were standard enough in this situation. If Frank was needled by this, so be it. 'What time did you finish work and set off for home?'

Frank gave him another filthy look, but his voice stayed steady. 'About half twelve.'

'Where did you say the school is?'

'It's in Linfrith. I didn't turn up a job around here.'

'Linfrith Academy?'

'I wish. St Egbert's. Its fees are low and it's not that well thought of. But then, neither am I.'

'And it takes you how long to reach home?'

'If I take the bus and it's on time, I get home about half one.'

Blades looked across at Frank's father, but his mother replied. 'He did get here at that time and we had lunch. Then Frank had marking and preparation to do. He didn't leave the house that afternoon.'

'He couldn't have gone out without your being aware of it?'

'I worked in my room,' Frank said.

'But your mother doesn't watch you all the time. You could have slipped away.'

'He didn't,' Frank's mother replied. 'We'd have heard him.'

'And we didn't hear him,' Alan said.

'I didn't go out,' Frank said.

'And why would you kill your fiancé anyway?' Blades said this in a light manner as if to suggest Frank would have no motive, but the way he left the question hanging might have suggested he wanted to know why Frank had.

'We were engaged. I wanted to marry her. Hardly the motivation for a murder,' Frank replied. The sentences were brief but the look in his eyes was eloquent.

'Quite so, sir,' Blades replied.

Blades supposed he had reached the end of his questions for Frank at the moment, particularly as, on the face of it, Blades didn't consider Frank a strong suspect. His mother could be capable of the crime, as she had such an obvious resentment of Daphne, but she had an alibi too.

'Thank you for your help,' Blades said. 'And once again, I'm sorry for your loss.'

Then he and Peacock took their leave. Blades noticed the look Frank gave him as he left, and he did think perhaps it was just as well Frank was a pacifist. As Peacock drove them off, Blades' mind still worked on Frank.

'You said you thought a conscientious objector could commit murder?' he said to Peacock.

Peacock's brow furrowed. 'Worn down and lashing out on the spur of the moment. I could see it. Yes. I did come across COs out in France. Field Punishment Number One. That's what they gave them. Have you heard of that?'

'No. What is it?'

'They would tie them to posts, or even a gun wheel, with their arms and legs stretched wide, just as if they were on a cross. With their feet just touching the ground and no more, so that their arms took all of the weight. It must have been hell. That was for the ones who wouldn't obey orders though. The ones in the Non-Combatant Corps wouldn't have been treated like that.'

'I wonder if Frank went straight into the Non-Combatant Corps. His father talked about someone called Clifford Allen.'

'If Frank was under his influence, I'm surprised he agreed to do anything at all for the war effort.'

'So, they could have made him suffer, he gave in, and agreed to join the Brigade.'

'It could have happened like that,' Peacock replied. 'And he would have still suffered even once he was in it. Another name for it was the No Courage Corps. Some of the rougher fighting men made a real point of having a go at them. Conchies were often set on when they were out and about.'

'And all those problems when he came back. That could make someone embittered.'

'He seems reasonably together – on the surface.'

Blades thought of some of the looks Frank Bywaters had given him when he was being questioned. He wondered just how dangerous Frank could be.

CHAPTER SIX

Blades was acutely aware of what Daphne's parents must be going through and wary of blundering in and upsetting them with insensitive questioning so that, when he did go to interview them again, he tried to use the lightest touch he could, which he soon thought may have been a mistake. As far as Marion Tanner was concerned, Inspector Blades wasn't setting foot in her place without being given a seat in her parlour and having tea and cake lavished on him. He must have been working ever so hard on the case and needed the chance to put his feet up for a moment, she said. Down-to-earth and working-class she might be, but she behaved with the courtesy of the aristocracy.

Putty in her hands, after tea duly arrived, Blades found himself seated beside Peacock and balancing a cup and saucer in his hands as he reached for the gingerbread, while wondering how to fit his official questions into the conversation. Marion would have talked about the weather for some time so that, when he did say, 'Can you tell me anything about what Daphne did on the day of her death?' he felt as if he had dropped a conversational clanger, but perhaps, he thought, in her heart of hearts, she knew she could not put off serious questions for ever.

It was Pete who replied. 'It was a normal day.'

'Which is?' Blades said.

Pete's look became confused and, the dullness of that day's weather mercifully forgotten, Marion took over. 'Daphne was at her work, just as Pete was, and I had my household chores to do.'

'And Robert?'

'He went out looking for work in the morning,' Pete replied. 'I forced him to. I get fed up of him hanging around the house feeling sorry for himself.'

'It must be difficult for him,' Blades said.

'He has to get on with building his life again. It won't do it by itself.' Pete paused and a weary expression came over his face. 'So, I suppose he went through the motions of that before going over to see Helen. He'd arranged to see her later.'

A silence gathered as Blades studied them and let his mind work on all of this.

'What are the things that Daphne usually does?'

Marion replied. 'Frank was often round, and she went out with him.'

'She saw Frank this week?'

'He was always round for tea on Monday. Chatting about his job and the children he works with.'

'Frank is always entertaining,' Pete said.

'And educational,' Marion added. 'You and he are always discussing books. Which one was it this week? HG Wells' *War of the Worlds*?'

'He continues my education. I enjoy it.'

'Pete was clever at school. He always wished he could have stayed longer but, when he was young, most people left school at ten years old, which was when he did.'

'So, I've always liked Frank and thought him a good sort for Daphne,' Pete said.

'If it wasn't for that conscientious objector business,' Marion said, interrupting him. Blades noted the indignant look she had given her husband as she said this. 'Half the neighbours won't speak to us now.'

'How did Robert get on with Frank?' Blades asked.

Neither Pete nor Marion spoke at first. Then Pete said, 'It was probably better to avoid having them both in the house at the same time.'

'Frank can't stop talking about politics,' Marion said.

'He's always on about the rights of the working classes,' Pete said. 'Myself, I like that from someone who isn't working class himself. It says something for him. And he hated the politicians who got us into that war. He goes on something dreadful about the way people suffered, and the money the industrialists made out of it while they sat miles behind the front lines themselves.'

'But it gets Robert mad,' Marion said. 'He tells Frank he ought to shut up. He's no right to talk like that when he didn't fight himself. I can see both of their points of view. I just wish they'd stop arguing about it.'

'One arm or not, Robert would have had a go at Frank if I hadn't stopped him,' Pete said. 'Not that he would have managed to do much, I suppose.' As he said this, his voice faded away and he looked into the fire.

'Poor Robert,' Marion said. 'He was such a hale and hearty young man before he went out there.'

'And it's how he still tries to behave, but he can't,' Pete said.

'So, he resented the fact Daphne was bringing Frank into the family?'

'I suppose he did,' Pete said.

'Not that he would hurt Daphne,' Marion said. 'He was very fond of his sister.'

'Of course,' Blades said, wondering at the need to point that out. Then a silence fell, and Blades took in exactly how defensive they were. He looked across at Peacock.

'He did make an effort with Frank,' Pete said. 'He'd have got over the fact he was a CO – in time.'

Then the silence returned.

'Did he argue with Daphne about him?' Blades asked.

'He was always good to his sister,' Marion said. 'He was older than her and she was a girl, but he was always good about spending time with her. And he would have defended her against anybody who treated her the wrong way.'

Blades noticed that his question had not been answered. 'How often did they argue?' he asked.

Marion opened her mouth to speak, then closed it again. She looked across at Pete, then continued. 'Not that much. Only when Frank had been around. Robert did tell her she ought to get rid of him. He would always be a chain around her neck and that of the family. But she defended her Frank. She was a stubborn girl, our Daphne.' Then Marion's face crumpled and, despite her best efforts, she started crying. Blades supposed she and Pete had been holding up bravely. It was only a couple of days since Daphne had been murdered and here was a policeman raking everything up.

Pete said, 'Robert's at a bit of a loss just now. He hasn't settled down since he came back. We all try hard to be patient with him. And Daphne was as well. Their rows didn't amount to much. Robert let off steam, that was all, and she pacified him mostly. Then he calmed down and forgot about it.'

'Did he and Daphne have any rows this week?'

'No,' Pete replied. 'What are you suggesting?'

Blades noted the tone had turned hostile.

'I'm just asking questions,' Blades said. 'Routine questions. When did Robert last see Daphne?' he asked.

'Not that day,' Marion replied, making a firm effort to pull herself together. 'He's never up when she leaves for work, and he wasn't here when she came back.'

'They were avoiding each other?' Blades asked.

'They got on all right,' Pete said, but his voice had risen.

'They weren't trying to keep out of each other's way,' Marion said, and there was a flustered look on her face. Blades was trying to work out what the row had been about between Robert and Daphne that week. 'They were both here at the evening meal the night before,' Marion continued, 'chatting about this and that, nothing of any consequence. Joking about Charlie Chaplin. Daphne had been to see one of his films and Robert was thinking of going.'

'No disputes?'

'It's not that sort of family,' Pete said. 'We get on with each other.' And that was said with an authority that was supposed to allow no argument, Blades thought.

'Of course,' Blades agreed. 'When was Frank last round here?'

'Last Saturday,' Marion said. 'Before he took Daphne out and after he brought her back.'

'Was Robert around then?'

'No,' Marion replied. 'He was out somewhere with Helen.'

'So, no rows with or about Frank recently?' Blades asked.

'No.' The look Marion gave Blades was now withering.

Blades considered her – and Robert. There was nothing evidential against him, and Blades supposed he had gained as much from that line of questioning as he would – for today, at least.

'I don't suppose she's seen any other young men lately?' he asked.

'Not for some time,' Pete said. 'She was taken with Frank.'

'Can you tell me who her girlfriends were?'

'There was Jane,' Marion replied.

'Jane who?'

'Jane Proudfoot. She worked in the same millinery store as Daphne. But Daphne hadn't seen her outside work for a while.'

'What was the cause of that?'

'Jane was jealous, as far as I could see,' Pete said.

'Jane wanted Frank herself, so she took to bringing up the fact Frank was a conchie to annoy Daphne. She was struck with him too, but Frank wasn't interested in her.'

'And she works at the same milliner's?' Blades asked.

'Yes.'

'I'll need to talk to her. She might be able to tell me if there was anything going on in Daphne's life she wasn't talking about at home.'

'Like what?' Marion said.

'I don't know,' Blades replied. He gave her a steadfast look.

'Maybe she would have been able to once,' Marion said. 'Not now. They had a row about Frank.'

'I see. And Daphne had other girlfriends?'

'There was Phyllis Drinkwater. They saw a lot of each other when they were at school. The war wore Phyllis down and they didn't keep up the same. But Daphne did make a point of seeing her now and again, as she felt she ought to give her some support. Phyllis lost her husband in the war and found herself left on her own with a child. She has a war pension which amounts to very little. She does live back with her parents and she takes in washing to help a bit with money. Her father is a cooper. He earns a good enough working man's wage, but that's not much. None of us are rich around here.'

'Had she been seeing Phyllis lately?'

Marion and Pete looked at each other. 'We don't know,' Marion said.

'No,' Pete said.

'Can you tell me how to get in touch with her?'

Then Marion told Blades the address.

'And we'd like to interview Robert again.'

'We'll let him know,' Pete replied.

Blades remembered the cup of tea that had loomed so large at the beginning of their meeting and took a sip. It was now, as could be expected, cold.

* * *

Robert arrived at the police station by himself this time. Blades wondered why Pete was not with him. He supposed Pete did not want to come across as overprotective, which could cast suspicion.

'You wanted to see me again?' Robert said after being shown into Blades' office. There was defiance in his tone.

'Yes,' Blades said, ushering Robert into a seat as Peacock reached for his notebook and pencil and joined them.

'Mother and father have been lecturing me,' he said. 'I have to give you my fullest co-operation. Establish my innocence.' He gave a bitter laugh. 'Anyway, here I am.' Then the smile left his face, leaving an angry stare.

Blades ignored all of this. 'You and Frank didn't get on, I believe?'

'How that helps your inquiries, I don't know. But no. I have no time for conscientious objectors. If everybody had pulled their weight in that war, it wouldn't have lasted so long and some of us might not have received our wounds.'

Blades wondered if petulance was ever absent from Robert's demeanour.

'Did you resent the fact your sister was going to marry a CO?'

Robert's eyes blazed. Then he allowed this to die away. 'I would hardly murder her because of that.'

Now Peacock joined in. 'Inspector Blades didn't suggest you did. These are background inquiries only.'

A sardonic laugh came from Robert. 'And it's obvious where they're going.'

Neither Blades nor Peacock replied to that. Then Blades said, 'How did you get on with your sister?'

'How does anyone?'

'You tell us, sir,' Peacock said.

Robert gave him a hard look, one which Peacock returned.

'I did tell her off for taking up with that Frank,' Robert said. 'He was oil and pretence. Him with his degree and his grand intellectual airs. He didn't have the gumption to join up and do his duty like everyone else. And what we have to put up with from other people because of him. I used to really like my Aunt Margaret. She took us out for great treats when we were children. And she gave us super presents. Then Daphne took up with Frank and she dropped us, not that I blame Aunt Margaret for that. She lost both her sons, and Frank is walking about happy as Larry.'

'So, you were at daggers drawn with your sister every time you met?'

Robert gave Blades an indignant stare. 'I don't know what that's supposed to mean, but it's not true. I always treated my sister properly.'

'Did you see her on Tuesday?'

'No. She was already at work when I got up and I'd gone out before she came back.'

'And did you see her the day before?'

'We did live in the same house. I saw her at mealtime, then went out.'

'Did you have a row with her then?'

'That's background information? No. I didn't kill my sister. Try finding the person who did.'

'So, you did have a row with Daphne?'

'No. I didn't.' Robert glared at Blades.

'The topic of Frank didn't crop up that time?'

Robert sighed. His stare at Blades was now weary. 'We spoke about nothing in particular. Isn't that what people talk about most of the time?'

Blades considered Robert. 'Have you had work since you came back?'

'My father managed to find me something. I did some clerical work for a while in an office. I could manage that with one arm.' And the self-pity was clear in his tone.

'So, how did that go?'

'Do you know what it's like when people are going out of their way to be kind to you all the time? Then, when they don't think you're watching, you see the looks of disgust as they stare at your empty sleeve.'

'So, you left?'

'That might have made sense. But I didn't. I went out of my way to avoid situations I didn't like, and even took days off to do that – too many. They decided I was an unreliable employee and dismissed me.'

'Which makes it even more difficult to find work.'

'Don't sugar it too much, Inspector.' Robert's voice was cutting. He looked as if he was going to explode but he managed some self-control. 'No. I haven't adjusted to civvy life since I came back. That doesn't mean I'm going to murder my sister.'

'Has someone in the locality been giving you problems over the fact Daphne was seeing a CO?'

Robert thought. 'Nobody in particular.'

'No one at all?'

'Just the odd snide comment when I'm out and about. I don't know what Daphne got. She didn't tell me.'

'So, most of the difficulties have been with your aunt?'

'And her husband. But they just dropped us.'

'We might talk with them.'

'They'll like that,' Robert said.

'What do you plan to do next in your life?'

In reply, Robert simply stared back, which Blades took to mean he did not know. Or it had been a question too far. He ended the interview by thanking Robert for coming in.

After he had left, Blades and Peacock discussed him.

'I like him for this murder,' Peacock said.

'He's a nasty piece of work,' Blades said, 'which is not the same thing. But he could have done it. His life's been destroyed, and it's left him bitter. He could take that out on someone if he was in enough of a tizzy.'

'Why that afternoon?' Peacock asked.

'His girlfriend had finished with him. He tried to walk off his temper about that, came across Daphne and just snapped. We need to talk to that girlfriend about him.'

* * *

Robert's girl, Helen Fallon, was a brunette with deep brown eyes and a dimple. Her face was plumpish but attractive. It was an open face; her eyes looked straight at the person she was talking to, and Blades found them on him now. He and Peacock were at her parents' house to interview her. It was an old building, one of the few left in the main street with a thatched roof. Helen's father was a joiner and Helen a lowly seamstress, yet the room they were in was fastidiously clean with brasses that gleamed, and Helen held herself with pride.

'I know Robert,' she was saying, 'and he wouldn't kill his sister.'

Blades pondered the reply. Helen must be feeling guilty about the position she had put Robert in when she finished with him. Not that he had accused Robert of murder, but the reasons for his questions were obvious. He continued.

'The police surgeon says that Daphne died at some time between two thirty and three thirty. Can you vouch for Robert being with you at that time?'

A flustered look appeared on Helen's face. 'I didn't look at the clock so, I don't suppose I can for all of that time.'

'But he was here as he said?'

'I don't know what he told you. I'll try to remember times. I might get them wrong. I'll try to get them about right.'

'As close as you can manage will do.'

'The conversation was dramatic. I ought to remember.'

'Dramatic? In what way?'

'If dramatic is the right word. I told him I was finishing with him and he didn't like it.'

'You had a row about it?'

'He objected and I told him what was what, I suppose, but it wasn't a violent argument. Anything but.'

'Had you been seeing him long?'

'About three years. We'd been engaged to be married at one point. If it hadn't been for the war, we would have wed, but I suppose you've heard that before.'

'It was common.'

'He was a fine young man before he went out there. Not always serious enough about things. But then what's wrong with having a light-hearted side to yourself? I wish he had one now. And you can't rely on him at all. He's completely unpredictable.'

Helen paused, as if embarrassed. Then she continued in a rush of words.

'It must have been dreadful losing his arm like that. And he was a tailor. He couldn't do his job anymore. I did stick by him all through the war, and then he came back like that. Other girls went on about how virtuous they were but went chasing after anyone when their men were away. I tried to do my best by him after he came back as well. I did. But he's—' Then, the words stopped. 'Maybe I'm harsh. I don't know. Maybe it's just me. But I've no time for self-pity. He feels too sorry for himself to do anything about anything. And he's so short-tempered with it. Do you know what I mean?'

'What kind of things annoy him?'

'It's not that. It's not that there are things that annoy him. He's just irritated inside himself, and it bursts out every so often at whatever. I can't see it coming. There's no reason for him getting bad-tempered that I can see. It's just something eating away at him and that has to come out.'

'That's difficult.'

'I decided I didn't want to live with that. Is that selfish of me? You hear about shellshock and it might be something like that, I suppose, and you should stick by them and maybe it'll just heal in time. It's what I should have done, isn't it?'

Blades said nothing.

'But it's not just that. He's never going to hold down a job again, and isn't that something a girl is looking for? Someone steady and reliable. A breadwinner?'

Again, Blades did not reply.

'If I hadn't found Colin, I suppose. But I did. And do you know what's worse? What I really love about Colin? He's got two arms. Isn't that a dreadful thing for me to say? Isn't it? But I'm young. I'm twenty-one. I'm healthy. I want a healthy young man. Am I not entitled to that? Why should the war take that away from me? What did I have to do with it? Did I start it?'

Then she stopped talking. She looked at Blades, then Peacock, then away. She bit her lip. She shifted in her seat. She looked back at Blades.

'I'm selfish, aren't I? That's what you're thinking?'

'Not at all,' Blades replied.

'But I am. And I can't help it. And what's more, I don't care that I am. I didn't mean to upset Robert. Really, I didn't. But he scares me. Did I say that? I'm frightened of him. He has hit me before. I know what you're thinking, that he's a one-armed man, but the arm he has is powerful enough. He can hurt you with it.'

Then she stopped talking again. She seemed to be looking inside herself and not liking what she saw. 'And he wasn't getting any better. All that hurt he brought back from the war. It wasn't going away.'

Blades continued with his questions. They had to be asked. He did try to put a gentle tone into his voice.

'So, can you say what time he arrived at your place and what time he left?'

The look Helen gave him was a bit frightened. 'I can't think,' she said. 'It's gone out of my head.' She thought for a moment. 'But he must have arrived at a bit after one. Not much. We had that long discussion and he stormed off. When? I didn't pay any attention, but it must have been after half two. Was it? Sometime between then and a quarter to three. I did look at the clock at that time and he had gone by then. So, I suppose that's about when he arrived and when he left. Was that helpful?'

'Very,' Blades said. 'You say he stormed off?'

'He didn't take it well. But he can't have gone off and done something like that. He can't, can he?' But Blades could hear the doubt in her voice. 'What did Daphne have to do with me finishing with him? I was the one who hurt him.'

'You're right,' Blades said.

As Helen had been helpful, Blades and Peacock were able to leave, feeling a reasonable amount of satisfaction, Peacock with his notebook placed neatly in his jacket pocket with all that precious information he had written down.

* * *

The milliner's where Daphne had worked was situated in the centre of Birtleby. It had a grand shop front with tall and wide windows, with pillars in a faux classical style. The signage was in gold lettering: Robertson's – Milliner's to the Gentry, though Blades supposed they would sell to anyone who entered.

Inside was an overwhelming display of hats on shelves, mostly in modern styles though there were still some of the Edwardian type. There were modern cloche hats in varied styles, colours and material, with different ribbon and embroidery finishes; in helmet style, in what looked like some sort of winged style, some prettified by flowers, some apparently inspired by the bold lines of the cubist fashion in paintings. There were broad-brimmed hats too: some were in straw, others in velvet, felt, wool, or silk, and in colour they ranged from the blush of pink to the brazenness of scarlet to the gentleness of lilac. Blades thought a young lady might enjoy working in such an establishment.

The young woman behind the counter smiled and asked if she could help. She was a tall, thin woman of a neat and clean appearance. She looked down-to-earth, a practical sort of person, and Blades thought that, if this was Jane Proudfoot, she might make a good witness. Blades showed his card and the young woman hesitated, then gave an uncertain smile.

'I want to talk with Jane Proudfoot,' he said. 'I understand she works here.'

'You're speaking to her,' Jane replied. 'How can I help?'

'We're investigating the death of Daphne Tanner. I believe you were a friend of hers.'

'We both worked here,' Jane replied, but did not add to that.

'You knew her well?'

Jane sighed. She thought for a moment. 'Not as well as I used to.' Then a regretful smile crept onto her face. 'She didn't have much to do with the likes of me after getting her posh boyfriend. Thought she'd gone up in the world, she did.'

'Frank Bywaters?'

'That's him.'

'You don't like him?'

'Why do you ask?'

'Just background inquiries,' Peacock said.

The same useful phrase, Blades thought. He must remind Peacock not to overdo that one. Jane gave Peacock a disbelieving look.

'It's a murder inquiry,' Blades said. 'You'd be surprised how much information we gather. You can't always tell what will be useful at the time. We make up our minds about that later.'

'I suppose,' Jane said, though her face was still full of suspicion. 'I'll answer your questions. What else am I going to do?'

'Thank you,' Blades said. 'How long have you known Daphne?'

'Since she started working here. A couple of years.'

'Did she have other boyfriends in that time?'

'She was struck with Frank.'

'What did you think about him?'

'He was a conchie. What else is there to say?'

'You don't like conchies?'

'Everybody hated them. They didn't do their bit.'

'Did that make you hate Daphne as well?'

'Hang on. I didn't say I hated Frank, just that lots of people did. I didn't care about him one way or the other.'

'You were good friends with Daphne once, weren't you?'

'Who have you been talking to?' She gave Blades a glare. 'Though I suppose I was. I did go off her because of Frank, but I didn't hate her or anything. I just stopped bothering with her. I couldn't see why she was interested in him.'

'You had quarrels with Daphne about him?'

'Frank's out of her league anyway. And mine. And I didn't like the way she got so stuck up about him.'

'Did you have a thing about Frank yourself?'

'Did I what?' She gave Blades another filthy look. 'Tongues around here,' she snorted. 'All right. I suppose you'll have it out of me. I did quite fancy him once. But then lots of blokes are attractive.'

'What was the quarrel with Daphne about?'

'There wasn't one. We drifted apart. That was all.'

'Did you?'

'Yes. All right. I did tell her what I thought about Frank's yellow streak. She said I was jealous, and we had a go at each other about that. She thought so much of herself because she had Frank – and he was in the No Courage Corps. It makes you laugh, that does. Those posh airs, and her with a father who's a postie. She's no better than me. Still, she wasn't that bad a sort. She didn't deserve to end up with her head bashed in on a beach. Why don't you go out and catch the maniac who did it, instead of asking me all these questions? Round up a few blokes and ask them.'

There were tender spots here, Blades thought, but he persisted with his questions.

'Do you know anything about Daphne's movements in the last week or so? Did she have any arguments with anyone? Had there been anyone strange in the shop?'

'We don't get men in here. And Daphne didn't tell me what she was up to. We weren't close any more. We hadn't even talked much in ages. We had to be polite to each other. We both worked here, but I didn't learn much about her private life. I was surprised she was found on the Ridges. I didn't think she would go there. Most of us girls avoid that place, even if all that stuff did happen a while ago. She might have gone out there with Frank, I suppose. But not on her own.'

'She wouldn't take the dog out there?' Peacock asked.

'She'd no control over that thing. I suppose it might have dragged her anywhere.'

'Dragged her?' Blades asked.

'The only spoiled one in that house is Pooky, great soft thing that he is. He just rushes off anywhere. She'd no control over him.'

'The only spoiled one?'

'I've no time for dogs myself. They're stupid, selfish things as far as I can see, but you should have seen the fuss they made over him. Dreadful if he did pull her out there though. She was letting him have fun and that's what happened to her?'

A pitying look came over her face. Blades and Peacock thanked her for her time.

* * *

Phyllis was in the washing-house at the back when Blades and Peacock arrived. This was a brick building separate from the house. Blades noticed the basic, metal-framed windows with cracks in one or two of the panes of glass. Once inside, he could see it had a stone floor, what looked like a wringer, a mangle, and a huge sink. Phyllis did not look displeased at being forced to stop in her task. She stood back from the wringer as soon as her eyes fell on them and wiped sweat from her brow. Blades thought she was probably only a year or two older than Daphne, but her skin was already starting to show signs of tiredness. Then she flashed a good-humoured grin and her face lit up.

'A couple of men dropping by to see what work looks like?'

Peacock repressed a laugh. Blades gazed across at the number of piles of washing waiting to be done.

'I do washing for other folks,' Phyllis said. 'It helps make ends meet. War widows' pensions are a disgrace.'

'Probably,' Blades agreed.

'Thanks for the excuse for a break, but what is it you want?'

Blades coughed to hide his embarrassment. He proffered his card. 'Allow me to introduce myself. I'm Inspector Blades and this is Sergeant Peacock.'

Phyllis inspected it. 'Do you have any idea who did it yet?' she asked.

'You're right. We're investigating Daphne Tanner's murder. You were a friend of hers I believe?' Blades said.

Phyllis did not reply at first but said instead, 'That was awful.' Her eyes clouded over. 'There have been too many awful things. What did you want to know?'

'Did you see her on the day she died, Tuesday?'

'No. We were close friends once, not so much now; though we still kept in touch. I'm kept busy, as you can see, and we'd grown apart anyway. Daphne was still young, single, and carefree.'

'That war left a lot of people with difficulties,' Blades said, 'which is a pity. Did you see her at any time in the week before her death?'

'I haven't seen Daphne for a couple of weeks. She did come around for a cuppa – when was it? Oh, about three weeks ago. She was her usual self, gossiping about work and besotted with Frank. A lot of folk thought he was a cross round her neck. I liked him myself, but I think he must have had an awful self-important streak to do what he did.' She paused as if considering her words and looked across at Peacock, as if in search of encouragement. 'You would have had to be like that to be a conchie, think the world of your own opinion; that, or be a downright coward, which Frank isn't. He thinks he's cleverer than he is, if you ask me, got himself into more trouble than he'd bargained for. But he has a way with him, Frank. He's all right. And he seemed to be coming out of things OK. Or so Daphne said. But then, she thought the world of him.'

'Frank and Daphne didn't quarrel? They were getting on fine?' Blades asked.

'They didn't have arguments that I know of. He was a lucky man that Frank. Having a girl like Daphne after what he did. He's not now, of course.'

'No.'

'Poor Daphne. It's dreadful to think of it. It– it was quick, was it?' She stopped talking and her anxious eyes stared at Blades now.

'Yes. I think he took her by surprise.'

'He didn't do anything else to her?'

'No.'

'That's a mercy. That's what every girl dreads. Dying's as bad as it gets, of course. But at least–' Then she ran out of words and looked away as she struggled with her emotions. 'I'm glad things weren't any worse for her.'

'What did Robert think of Frank?'

'Robert's been a misery about everything since he came back. Not that I blame him. It was dreadful, what happened to him. How do you get over that? Daphne worried about him. He's so bitter.'

'Did Robert give Daphne a difficult time?'

'Robert wouldn't have killed her, though I expect he did give her a hard time now and again. He gives everyone problems. He never stops picking arguments. And he didn't used to be like that. Or nothing like as bad, anyway. He did have a go at Daphne about Frank. You'd think sometimes it was Frank's fault Robert lost his arm. If Frank had done his bit – and all the rest of them – we'd have rolled the Germans over in about two weeks, the way Robert speaks about it. Rubbish, of course. I don't think much of a man for not going out there, but there weren't that many conchies. Of course, someone like that isn't someone you'd want to depend on, but there was no telling Daphne that.'

'And you were where, on Tuesday afternoon?'

'Here.'

'No one turned up asking for Daphne?'

Phyllis gave Blades a puzzled look.

'Apart from my mother, my daughter, and a pile of washing, I didn't see anybody or anything.'

'Thank you.'

'Why do you ask?'

'You don't know anybody else who might have been on the beach at the same time as Daphne that afternoon, then?'

'Wait a minute. I did see someone. But he wasn't asking after Daphne. It was just a tramp. He came by and begged. It was someone I've never seen before, but it could be some stranger who did this, couldn't it?'

'We consider all possibilities.'

'You ask about Robert and Frank as if they're prime suspects and I know them; I can't imagine either of them doing anything like this.'

'You're suspicious of this tramp? Why?'

'I don't know that I am, but he was an evil looking fellow and someone killed her.'

'Did he talk about her?'

'He didn't talk about anything. He was just after the makings of a meal. We've enough problems feeding ourselves, but Mam took pity on him. You can rely on her doing that.'

'What did he look like?'

'If you've seen one tramp you've seen them all. He was about average height. Let's see. About five nine. Average sort of smell for a tramp, I should think. It's their feet, I suppose. All that walking about from casual ward to casual ward. I didn't notice anything special about his face. His nose and ears didn't stick out. He didn't have any scars. He was really weather-beaten, if that helps. Though I suppose they all are. The way he spoke was maybe a bit odd. He had a pleading, whining sort of voice. He'd a northern accent, much the same as anyone else's around here. He did stop moaning and simpering after he'd got out of Mam what he could. He was smug then, even rude. He was dressed in an old overcoat – and in shocking trousers. All ragged at the bottom, they were. He had good sturdy looking boots, or they would have been. They'd seen better days.'

'Did he give a name?'

'We weren't that friendly with him. Who knows what a tramp's going to get up to?'

'Did he say where he was heading for?'

'He mentioned something about Fossmouth. He did say he'd spent the night in the casual ward here and was getting ready to set off. He looked the bad-tempered sort, a bit worn down if you know what I mean. It might be worth checking up on him.'

'Would you recognize him again?'
'Oh yes. Definitely.'

CHAPTER SEVEN

Blades was standing in the police station in front of a display of photographs and notes on the case so far. He supposed the look on his face was a bit grumpy, and he tried to put on an air of professional seriousness instead. Seated in front of him were several rows of constables and sergeants.

'This is the information on the case so far,' Blades was saying. 'We have made progress, mostly consisting of establishing different possible lines of inquiry. There are similarities to the Ridges murders, the first being where she was killed. There was the trademark brushing away of footprints. The victim is similar in age and gender. The method of murder was the same: death by a blow or blows. The major difference is the rock was carried some way off this time, though we did locate it eventually, unhelpfully without useful fingerprints. And the body was not buried. Although we have been looking at the old case files, it's difficult to see pointers that help.

'It's possible this is a murder done by a different person for a different reason but done in such a way as to suggest it was done by the same maniac who did the others. So, following that line of inquiry, we ask ourselves who amongst Daphne's friends and relations might have killed her?'

A hand was raised in the front row. 'The boyfriend?'

'Whose name is Frank Bywaters. He's a conscientious objector, which suggests he wouldn't be a useful line of inquiry, as he doesn't believe in killing people. That is his problem, or is supposed to be, and, when interviewed, he does come across as a reasonable, level-headed sort of person. But of course, the war did put everyone's personalities under strain, and a lot of people made a point of making sure that conscientious objectors did suffer, and still do. A conscientious objector gone wrong might be capable of this, but with Frank there is no sign of mental instability.'

'So, we dismiss Frank Bywaters as a suspect?' another constable asked.

'For the moment, at least.'

'Her family?' someone else asked.

'Her brother, Robert Tanner, is someone under mental strain. He's definitely damaged both physically and mentally. In interviews, he is combustible and bitter. He has had employment problems since he came back from the war because of the loss of his arm. On top of which, his girlfriend finished with him that day – and she says she's afraid of him. She talks of unpredictable violence. After their bitter argument that day, Robert Tanner stormed off, and there are no witnesses so far to his movements after that. He admits to being in the beach area, and it would have been possible for him to be on the Ridges at about the time of the murder, though he doesn't admit to that.'

'Why don't we arrest him?' a voice called out.

'Evidence. We haven't got any. As he is a strong suspect, trying to find proof against him is a priority in inquiries. Witnesses who can place him on the Ridges at the time of the murder would be ideal. Door-to-door inquiries might flush some out.

'Some witnesses have come forward in response to the newspaper report. A couple was spotted thereabouts. A tramp was seen. A suspicious car was parked nearby. There was an ex-soldier selling shoelaces. A drunk man loitered about in that area. But we do need names for these people so that we can bring them in for questioning so, be vigilant in those door-to-door inquiries. We could try another newspaper article which would turn up the usual amount of irrelevant 'helpful' information and mean we would have to spend a lot of time sifting through it, so I favour door-to-door questioning at the moment. Robert was obviously somewhere, and someone must have seen him there.

'If we could turn up the mysterious tramp who was mentioned by more than one person, that would be extremely useful. You never know. It might not have been Robert who did this. He's just a strong suspect. It could have been this unknown vagabond.'

One of the constables spoke. 'The Ridges murders, particularly the last one. Could a tramp have been involved there?'

'Tramps were interviewed then,' Blades said. 'We could try to establish if they were in the area this time. We will go to the casual ward and make inquiries there.'

'Did Daphne have other boyfriends?' It was Sergeant Ryan who spoke this time.

'We're told not,' Blades replied. 'She was struck with Frank.'

'Did anyone show any unwanted interest in her?' Ryan asked.

'Not that we know of.'

Then silence fell as Blades looked round the room again, waiting for more questions. He spoke again. 'This is of particular concern to the young women in the neighbourhood. Can they go about in safety or not? We need to catch whoever did this. Pull out all the stops to find out as much as you can. And when you are interviewing young women, do ask them if they have received unwanted attention from men. Has anyone alarmed or frightened them?'

Blades finished and there was a lot of coughing and chatter, and the sound of seats shifting as men stood up and moved around.

CHAPTER EIGHT

It was late evening when Blades and Peacock arrived at the casual ward. Blades supposed the porter would be used to visits from the police, as he knew a sergeant did sometimes call to inspect the men and see if there was anyone there of interest. The porter, whose name Blades discovered was Stan Levington, unlocked the door to the ward and switched on the light.

There must have been over twenty men there, Blades supposed, as he looked at the heads that stirred from under their blankets. The faces looked bewildered and angry. Blades flicked his eyes round them. He noted there were no bunks for the men in this ward, the men having to sleep on the floor. The single item of furniture was a sanitary bucket for the night's convenience. Blades was surprised the smell in the room was not more rank, but it was early yet, and he knew that these men would have been forced to wash on entry when their clothes were taken from them and the uniform nightshirt handed out. So, even if a better description had been given of the way the tramp had been dressed, this would not have helped just now.

Blades' eyes continued to glance over the men. There was a variety of humankind here; amongst them, youths who looked only about sixteen but who, Blades knew, would have pretended to be eighteen to claim the rights of that age. One man, who must have been about forty, had a long flowing beard of a fineness that suggested it had never seen a razor. He gave Blades a good glower from knowing eyes. There were some large frames, but all the men seemed to sag. None of them looked as if they had eaten well in some time. Their faces had a uniform haggardness and they possessed a downtrodden air, as if they had seen everything that life could throw at them. Despite that, they looked defiantly at Blades. What right did the law have to walk in here and spoil their rest?

'Were any of you in the area last Tuesday?' Blades asked.

Levington spoke at this point. 'It would be unlikely. They're allowed to stay one night before moving on.'

'Where to?'

'The next spike.'

'The next casual ward?' Blades asked.

'As I said. Some head over Fossmouth way, some towards Linfrith, some towards Marchbank.'

'I was here on Tuesday,' one voice claimed, 'not that I stayed in the spike that night. But I was in Birtleby.'

'You must like Birtleby,' another voice said. 'I wouldn't stay in the place for more than a night.'

'The best class of slop bucket to be found anywhere,' the first replied, and cackled.

Blades looked at him with interest. If the man known why Blades had asked the initial question, he would not have answered, so Blades presumed he had not done the murder.

'Did you walk along the shore road?'

'For a bit of the sea breeze?' the man hooted. 'I might have done at that. Why?'

'And your name is?' Blades asked.

'What do you want to know that for?' A look of belligerence was now on his face. 'What it's always been. Len.'

'Did you go anywhere near the Ridges?'

'Reckon I did.' As there was still no anxiety on Len's face, Blades supposed he did not keep up with the newspapers.

Peacock whispered to Blades. 'It could have been him she saw.'

'Who could have been me?' Len said, worry in his voice now.

'Did you see anything out of the ordinary?' Blades asked.

'Like what?'

'Something you wouldn't expect to see?' Peacock said.

'I've no idea what you mean.'

'Then you probably didn't,' Blades said. 'But if you did notice a young woman being attacked, it would help us.'

'Someone was attacked?' Len said. He looked alarmed. 'Are you accusing me of something? I didn't do anything to any young woman.'

'Did you see one?'

'I would have had the sense to walk off somewhere else if I had. What would any young woman want with me?'

'Len wouldn't do anything,' a voice called out.

'Leave him alone. He's not done anything,' another one said.

A general muttering broke out.

'He's not being accused,' Blades said. 'We just want his help. Len, did you notice a young woman anywhere along the Ridges on Tuesday afternoon?'

'I make a point of never noticing anything,' Len said. 'It gets you into trouble.'

The first voice spoke again. 'He does too. Let him be.'

'Len's not going to answer any questions in here,' Peacock said.

'How would you like to spend the night in a proper bunk?' Blades said.

'What do you mean?' Len answered.

'We've much more comfortable billets in the station,' Blades said.

'You can arrest me too if you like,' someone else said. 'The grub can't be any worse than it is in here.'

'Jammy bugger you are, Len,' another voice piped up. 'Think of us when we're chopping wood in the morning in return for our uncomfortable night's kip.'

'I saw a young woman on the Ridges,' a young bearded tramp volunteered.

'Not on Tuesday you didn't,' Peacock said.

'Yes, I did. I was lying earlier on.'

'And she was with your inspector,' a wag added, which led to general laughter.

Peacock helped Len to his feet, and they left the sleeping room behind.

'Do you have a record of the men who stayed here on the Tuesday night – and the Monday?' Blades asked the porter.

'I can give you the names they gave me,' he replied. 'It's an offence to give a false one but that's what half of them do, so, how much help it will be to you, I don't know.'

'They're supposed to tell you where they're heading when they leave here, aren't they?'

'They make something up, but they often don't know themselves. If good begging chances turn up somewhere else, they'll head off there.'

'So, it won't do us a lot of good to try to track down tramps who could have been around here on Tuesday.'

'You might manage to track some of them down. But they could be anywhere by now, even though they do travel on foot, at any of the other casual wards in the district, that is. That's where they head. But getting them to tell you if they were here on Tuesday? Good luck with that one. I was surprised you got so many answers out of Len.'

'We can do line-ups. We have witnesses,' Peacock said.

'You could try that,' Levington said.

* * *

They did attempt it. There was no shortage of tramps to pick for the line-up, though finding enough of the right height and age took time. In addition, they had a couple of policemen don disreputable rags. Mrs Randall picked out Len as the one who had been following Daphne, which brought the expected protestations. Jane chose a tramp who was verified to have been in Mossbank workhouse that evening, too far for him to have walked in that time, so they were missing one down-and-out, the one who had been at Jane's house.

When Len found himself facing Blades and Peacock, he wriggled about, protested, simpered, and looked generally alarmed.

'I was only walking the same way. As it happened. It's not against the law to walk somewhere. Why is it always the homeless who get picked on when something happens? There's always a police sergeant down at the casual ward, asking us questions, and we haven't done nothing. If we were any good at committing crimes, we'd have a roof over our heads.'

'You'd be surprised how often the culprit does turn up in a casual ward,' Blades said.

'It wasn't me.'

'So you say.'

'I've been caught out nicking things some shopkeeper had left lying outside his shop. I admit that. Do you know what they give you to eat in casual wards? Bread and cheese. I ask you. It's enough to turn anyone into a criminal. If someone's a bit careless in leaving their potatoes sitting outside, how am I to know they've not been left out for the poor anyway?'

'They're for sale,' Blades said.

'You don't know what it's like.'

Blades watched Len fidget on his seat. 'This isn't about the theft of a potato.'

Len squirmed about more but said nothing. He looked at Blades with a pleading expression. He glanced at Peacock but saw no sympathy there either. Then he looked down at the floor.

'We have a witness who says you were on the shore at Birtleby, walking behind Daphne Tanner, on the afternoon she was murdered. What do you have to say about that?'

'Murdered, did you say?' Len furrowed his brow then said, 'I don't know.' He looked around him in alarm, as if looking for a way out. 'I wouldn't do anything like that. I wouldn't.'

Blades and Peacock continued to stare at him as they waited for a proper answer.

Then Len said, 'All right. I did see a young woman. Was it Daphne Tanner? It wasn't someone I know, and I didn't pay her much attention. Quite short, slim with a quick, easy walk on her. Fawn jacket and hat. Brown curly hair. Was that her? But she was OK the last time I saw her.'

'That's a good description of someone you didn't pay much attention to,' Blades said. 'Why did you have such a good look at her?'

'Why did I what?' A flustered look appeared on Len's face. 'Why wouldn't I notice an attractive young woman walking along? I'm a man, aren't I? Wouldn't you?'

'You were attracted to her, so you followed her. What were your intentions?'

'I didn't say I followed her. We were going the same way. Don't you listen?'

Blades and Peacock said nothing as they waited again for him to continue.

Len looked back at Blades and Peacock. If possible, he was starting to look even more desperate. 'I was heading out to Fossmouth. That was all. Then she turned off along the track to the Ridges and I lost sight of her. That dog of hers took her out there. It had seen a rabbit or something I think, and that dog could run. And she chased after it. I don't think I could have caught up with them if I'd wanted to. It takes me all my time to get from one spike to the next.' He looked from Blades to Peacock with mournful eyes.

'This sounds possible,' Blades said. 'Did you see anyone else?'

'You believe me.' A beaming smile appeared on Len's face. 'Hallelujah.'

Blades repeated his question. 'Did you see anyone?'

Len frowned. 'Now I think of it, there was someone else there. He came along afterwards and turned off on the path that leads to the Ridges too, not that I watched him do that. And I didn't go along there. But yes. There was someone else around.'

'What did this person look like?'

'I dunno. What was he like? I didn't look at him. A medium-sized fellow. Thin. Yes. He was thin. Didn't look like your usual great hulking murdering maniac. Not that I've met any. A bit of a sour look on his face, though. And he was fairly striding along, as if in a real tizzy about something or other. I don't think he noticed me.'

'Did you recognize him?'

'Recognize him? Probably wouldn't know him from Adam if I saw him again. Except. Oh yes. I did say, didn't I? He only had one arm. The sleeve on his right arm was tied back. It was empty.'

'He'd one arm?' Blades said.

Peacock looked up from his notebook. His mouth hung open.

It was Robert Tanner, and as good a description as you could get. Len had placed Robert exactly where he said he had not been, walking towards the Ridges. Why would

Robert lie about that? The obvious reason presented itself to Blades.

* * *

Peacock agreed with him. They discussed it after releasing a grateful Len, to whom they had stressed their need to be able to keep track of him.

'When he was in a bit of a temper, which he was, and had an argument with his sister – which he may have done – that's when Robert could have done this,' Blades said.

Peacock nodded.

'He could have lashed out,' Blades continued. 'And if he's done it once, he could have done it before.'

'He might be our Ridges murderer?'

'If we were right about Pulteney, he couldn't have done all of them.'

'But he could have murdered Elspeth?'

'The third Ridges victim,' Blades said.

Peacock nodded. 'Yes. Not that I interviewed him at the time, but one of the sergeants did. Robert's name didn't come up in connection with Anne Talbot or Jane Dawson, but it did arise in connection with Elspeth Summers. He was an occasional customer in the Victoria, where she worked. A lot of people frequent that public house and he was just one of the many. Reports didn't show him even having spoken to her apart from ordering drinks, but we were thorough. We did question him – and dismissed him.'

'Who did the questioning?'

'One of the sergeants. At the time, we were following the theory that the three murders were all committed by the same man. Probably because that's what was all over the press. "Birtleby Police Bungle. They hang the wrong man".'

'But if we look at who Elspeth and Daphne might have known in common?'

'Robert Tanner assumes more significance.'

The two men pondered this. 'Tell you what, Peacock,' Blades said. 'You look over those files again. See if there's anything else in common there.'

'Yes, sir.' Peacock departed to the archives, leaving Blades to his thoughts.

It had been a difficult time just after this war, and, as a consequence, there were a lot of strange men around, Robert definitely being one of them. But this still needed to be properly considered. That did not mean he was a murderer. To lose his arm was difficult, and his trade, and his girl. But how strong were the grounds for suspicion? A witness placed him there. What kind of witness would Len present himself as on the witness stand? Not one who would give a jury confidence. The case would hinge on the impression Robert made on them, a better one than Len, Blades would be prepared to bet, so why were they continuing with this line of inquiry? But Robert would still be questioned.

And the murder of both Elspeth and Daphne? Did Blades think Robert had that in him? He considered Elspeth. Why would Robert kill her? They knew he had met her. There was no reason to suppose he knew Barker and Nuttall, the first two suspects, even if he did drink in the same place from time to time, and there was no reason to suppose he knew Pulteney, but there was a tenuous connection with Elspeth. What was she like? A bit of damaged goods herself by all accounts, if not physically. Robert could resent her as she did not have to serve on the front line – but no more than he did any other woman. Or was he attracted to her only to find himself rebuffed because of that empty sleeve? He could have had some twisted reaction to that. Blades thought back to the flame-haired body of Elspeth on that beach. Did Robert do that? Maybe, but it would be awful to arrest Robert and then find him innocent, after all he had gone through. Then, there was what they would be putting his parents through at a time when they had just lost their daughter. Blades would go carefully here.

Despite that, the possibility Robert Tanner was the murderer had to be taken into account. Blades had seen the flash of temper in him when questioned. It was possible he had reached killing point. Daphne could have said something to him. What? Robert would have been complaining about the way Helen had let him down. She had made him furious when she had finished with him. What would Daphne's reaction have been to that? Sisterly sympathy? Or did she lose patience with his self-pity and his inability to see what other people were going through? Would that have brought him to such a boiling point? Blades was not sure it would have done, unless Robert had committed murder before. A flash of temper. A flash of memory of how he had eased such anger in the past. Then, before he knew what he had done, his sister was lying in front of him, dead. After that, what? On the spur of the moment, Robert tried to make some attempt to make it look like the Ridges murders, so that the conclusion drawn would be that some homicidal maniac had done the murder, not someone who knew Daphne. The body was in the right place. What was there to do? He managed to think of sweeping the footprints away. All he had to do was scuff those away with his feet. He ought to have left the blood-covered rock behind. Why didn't he? Did he not realise it was still in his hand and throw it away later when he did? If Robert had any sense, he would deny all of this and the police would have to come up with proof. They would need to track down more plausible witnesses. Robert must have had blood on his clothes, of course. Yes. That was something to follow up on.

CHAPTER NINE

A phone call from Birtleby workhouse interrupted Blades at that point. It was the porter at the casual ward, Levington. There had been gossip amongst the tramps and a lot of them had been speaking up for Len. The porter wanted to know if they were going to charge Len with murder. Blades wasn't surprised at casuals sticking together, as it was what they did when the police questioned them.

'I know Len,' Levington said. 'We're on his circuit so he does turn up here every so often. He's quite stable, unlike a few of them. He likes life on the road. He never causes any bother in the spike. Nothing goes missing when he's around.'

'He's convincing then,' Blades replied. 'We'd noticed that.'

'You're not saying he murdered the girl, not Len?'

'No,' Blades said. 'He persuaded us too. We're letting him go, but we want to keep in touch with him. I know you usually only allow your visitors to stay one night, but it would be useful if we knew where Len was.'

'You found out something from him?' Levington asked.

'Possibly. Or not. It's still to be established.'

'We could offer him more than one night if it's of help to you – or do you want us to detain him? There's usually nothing to stop them wandering off after they've done their chores in the morning.'

'We're just asking him to stay in the area,' Blades said.

'Right you are. There's one more thing.' The voice at the other end of the phone paused at this point as if bothered by something. Then it continued. 'I heard the men gossiping amongst themselves. They wouldn't inform on each other. The world's against them, including me by their way of it, but I know you're looking for a murderer, so I keep my ears open. There is somebody on the road they're scared of.'

'Who's this?'

'He goes by different names – like a lot of the tramps who pass through.'

Blades could imagine that to be true of the type of person the porter dealt with. 'You're sure they're all talking about the same man?'

'A good question. I don't know.'

'So, tell me about him anyway.'

'He has a bit of a way with him, in the same way that Len does. He's a likeable enough soul, so everyone else seems to find. Harmless you'd think too, except that, just when you're thinking that, he changes. A few of them have been beaten up by him. In various places, down Leeds way, over at Harrogate, up at Halford, at Linfrith, at Fossmouth.'

Blades began to wonder why Levington was giving any credence to the idea this was all one person. 'He seems very busy with his fists.' Blades said.

'He could be a story, for all I know. It's just what they say.'

'A legend of the road. So, what's he supposed to look like?'

'That's another odd thing. They say they would recognize him anywhere but, when you ask them to describe him, he could be like anybody. Height? Let's see, about average, they say. Hair colour. Dunno. Oh, that would be brown. The same as most people's. And you'll want to know what his face was like. The same as most people's, according to them. Nothing that stands out. No odd-sized ears or anything like that. Features, sort of regular.'

Levington paused again on the other end of the phone as if embarrassed. 'He's not sporting any scars anywhere with all those fights he gets into?' Blades asked.

'He's not the one who's on the receiving end.'

'Is he thin, fat, muscular, or what?'

Levington laughed. 'I asked them that too. About average build.'

'That's not much help either.'

'Not a lot. And the colour of his eyes? One person says brown, another says grey, another green, another black, another grey. Take your pick.'

'Do you know the names he goes under?'

'Alex in one place, Alex Martin apparently, John Cross in another, or was it John Hope, Chris something somewhere else, then Jimmy something, and Peter something. He's probably got more monikers than I've had hot dinners.'

'What makes them say it's the same person?' Blades asked.

'Whoever it is always behaves in exactly the same way. Chats away like normal, then seems to withdraw and go off somewhere else entirely.'

'Like where?'

'A good question. He mutters to himself. He paces about. He disappears into his own thoughts and loses track of who he's with. He rants about the war. You might think he was back in the trenches again. He's got a thing about rats, giant rats. And he argues – with people who aren't there. Then switches out of that, and it's as if he's back to normal. That's when he turns on the person he's with, and beats him to a pulp.'

'Nice fellow to know,' Blades said.

'To avoid. They do their best to stay out of his way, and they warn each other about him.'

'Has he been around here?'

'He has been.'

'Do you know when?'

One of the porter's pauses occurred, and Blades wondered what he was going to hear at the end of it.

'The word is he was around at about the time that girl was killed on the beach.'

'Did you see him then?' Blades asked.

'He might have been in the ward. Or not. That description didn't help me much.'

'Was there someone here under the names they suggest?'

'There often is. Doesn't mean it's him.'

'How do they know he was here?'

'You might ask.' Now Levington spoke with a worried certainty. 'But they're convinced. That's all I know.'

Blades gave this some thought. 'I'm not sure I buy this,' he said. 'It sounds like a rumour. There might or might not even be such a person. There are a lot of people going around damaged by that war, and some of them could be in that state, or something like it. So, a legend grows up about this super-bad tramp who fits all these different people who behave like that. Someone is killed here, so it must have been him. But the reason they can't give a name or a proper description is because he doesn't exist. He's a story.'

'Still, I thought I would pass it on.'

'Quite right too,' Blades said. 'I'm grateful for your time and I won't ignore it. I'll send a sergeant and constable up to interview your gentlemen.'

82

'Who'll be long gone by now and we'll have a different lot in again.'

'Still, the new bunch might have heard about the same man, and we can look at your list of names of the tramps who told you about this and see where they said they were heading to.'

That was the end of the telephone conversation with the porter. Blades discussed it with Peacock. Apart from anything else, it allowed him to mull over what he had been told.

'You don't believe it?' Peacock said.

'The passing tramp theory? I'm not fond of it. I'm not saying it couldn't have happened. I still think it's more likely to have been someone who knew her, someone with a connection we can find out about and a motive, even if it is irrational.'

'A lot of these tramps fought in the trenches. They were trained to kill.'

'I don't dismiss the tramp theory.'

'You just think it's Robert?'

'He's our best lead at the moment.'

CHAPTER TEN

The girl the newspapers say was found killed: wasn't that the one I followed? I was there. She died. I must have done it again. I can't argue with that. That easy way she walked, that sense of peace in the way she flicked her hair: I killed that?

It was why I left before, to escape from doing such things, to break free of myself by tramping to another place, another spike; the only relief, the ache of limbs at the end of the day. I wanted to walk the anger off. After I reached the spike, I was another casual in the queue and, when they took my clothes away, the loss of self was almost complete. When I cleansed myself in the communal bath before putting on the workhouse garb, I became someone else, someone without the agony for a moment or two at least. I was another tramp amongst the rest sleeping on the floor. But I couldn't help thinking. A casual ward in a workhouse with bread, gruel, and cheese to sup on: I came back from the trenches for this?

What I never escaped was the smell of cordite and the scream of shells. They returned every night. Once again, the earth shook beneath the thunder of the guns, and I felt the coldness of mud under my hand and the squelch of it under my feet. Every night, they fought out in those trenches again, the ones in my head. It's some time since the war stopped, except it never did, just as the fear never went away. I huddle in that funk-hole every night, listening to the sound of artillery. Then, I become tired of being afraid, and the anger comes back. Anger: is that all I am now?

In the morning, I put my clothes back on with the fleas in them — the ones that were already there and the ones that came from the other clothes in the pile from the other casuals — and set off to try to tramp off my rage again.

After that other girl was killed, I had left Birtleby again, but the place owned my soul and I had to come back to find it. My thoughts turn to that girl, as they often do. Who was she? A fine afternoon and there she was, on the Ridges, walking by herself, apart from that dog. Why would she do that? Didn't she know the danger she was in?

Now, I wander the town again, everything the same, except it isn't. Night-time, and I am wandering in the direction of the shore, when I come across her. This young woman is tall and thin, unfettered in the way she holds herself. That speaks to me. I want to own that lightness of soul. I follow her. I always follow them. It never helps. I can watch that innocence in the face as the light catches it; I can study it; I can worship it; but I can't own it. I can walk in her footsteps, but I can't share them. I want to reach out with my hand and grasp that purity, but it will never be mine. Why should it be hers?

As I continue to follow her, she doesn't turn around. She should. They should. Someone walking behind her, never slower, never faster: she should notice that. She should listen for it, so that she can heed its warning, but she doesn't. When she reaches the light of a gas lamp, she turns right and disappears. That was a good trick. Where did she go? When I walk further on, I see it, the lane leading downhill with the high walls on either side of it. As she entered it, she left the light behind her and I can't see her, but she must be there. Should I follow her into that darkness? This is Birtleby. This is what I do here. The lane beckons; she beckons. I walk on and enter the alley. For tonight, this is where I am, and where my anger is, and I will do what it tells me.

CHAPTER ELEVEN

The body-count was mounting up again, Blades was thinking. Another young woman, and in her early twenties. The body type was different. This one was tall and thin with little curvaceous about her. And she had not been killed on the Ridges, nor even on a beach, but in an alley with the odd name of the Khyber Pass: a narrow, steep flight of steps between houses. She had been discovered by a man on his way to work in the early morning. They had sealed off the alley now, and if anyone else wanted to take a shortcut, they would have to go a different way.

Blades stood with Peacock beside the body, looking down at the woman's spread-eagled remains. The face was intact, at least. This young woman had not been battered by a rock. She had been stabbed – more than once at that – and blood lay in pools around her. As Blades studied the face, he realised he recognized this one. It had been a handsome face, if thin, with high cheekbones and the recently fashionable make-up showing she had pride in herself, Blades supposed: the use of powder careful, the pink lipstick not lurid but pale, hinting at something aspirational. Yes. He had come across her that once.

What had brought her down this lane? Blades supposed she was dressed for an evening out. Her jacket held a sleek look to it, and the hat was stylish and fur-trimmed. But how did she come to be by herself in such a gloomy alley – if she had been by herself? Blades pondered what the lane connected. The upper part led to the Marchmount area. At the bottom of its slope, it widened out as it joined the High Street and the main area of the town. Blades supposed she must have been out for the night somewhere and had been walking home, which meant she was probably walking up the slope towards the Marchmount area.

If she was with someone, who might that have been? Blades wondered if a young woman on her own would enter that alley. It was bounded by the walls of adjacent properties, it was not overlooked, and it was badly lit. Whoever this young woman had been with, had done this. Some man no doubt – they might be able to find out who that was. They could find out who was in her social circle. It was tragic to see another young woman lying there as a corpse. She had been in the flush of youth with so much to look forward to, but Blades could not allow his mind to dwell on that. He had the logistics of the investigation to work out.

A flashbulb popped and drew Blades' eyes away from the corpse and over to where Peacock stood with his camera.

'This is a narrow lane,' Blades said. 'You'd be better to wait till you have the chance to be in here on your own.'

'Of course, sir,' Peacock replied.

'Do you recognize her?' Blades asked.

Peacock looked down at the body. 'Is that–?' he said. 'Oh, yes, it is.'

'Next question,' Blades said. 'Is this in any way like our Ridges murders?'

'No.'

'Does it hold any similarities at all to the murder of Daphne Tanner?'

'Another young woman lying dead of unnatural causes in Birtleby?' Peacock suggested.

'There is that.'

'Her skirt is swept back. Could this one have been interfered with?'

'That would be a departure. No doubt, Parker will tell us.' Blades continued to stare at the body. 'One on the beach and one in the town. One battered with a rock and one stabbed. That does suggest someone else except – I suppose there wouldn't have been rocks to hand in an alley. We could consider whether it was the same person.'

'He must have brought the knife. Was there planning this time?'

'A good question.'

'Why choose this place?'

'Was it the victim he was choosing?' Blades asked. 'Did he know she would come up here? Or did he bring her?'

Peacock frowned. 'The Ridges murders were committed by someone on their own, with a young woman in a vulnerable place, who seized an opportunity, whether it was someone he knew or someone he followed. This is the same thing. She was passing through a lonely spot for whatever reason and he took advantage of it.'

'If this was the same murderer as Daphne's, that might have been planned too. We need to know who could have been in the area of both murders.'

'We need witnesses.'

'We always do.'

Blades looked up from the corpse, and his eyes swept up the lane. 'Take your photographs, Peacock,' Blades said, then wandered further up the Khyber Pass, his eyes moving from side to side as he perused the cobbles for anything that might have been left behind. A cigarette end interested him, and he picked it up and bagged it. Hadn't there been the end of a Turkish cigarette at the previous crime scene? It was Peacock who had noticed that, and it would be amongst the scene-of-crime evidence. Blades continued scanning the alley till he reached the top of it, where it met with the street as it led further uphill. There were houses on either side that had views of anyone entering the alley – or leaving it. Constables could make their door-to-door inquiries here. Something might have been spotted, even someone behaving oddly. A man running would be useful. A murder was about to be committed or had just been, and someone must have been in a state of nervous excitement about that.

Blades walked slowly back down the alley, eyes still moving everywhere, taking in as much as they could, till he came across Peacock still busy with his camera. Dr Parker was there now, with that shiny black leather bag, and the supercilious sneer that showed no feelings. Blades did not envy doctors their job. How did they cope with so many corpses? As a policeman, Blades encountered fatalities too, but it was not the normal course of things. Most crimes did not involve murder. Thank God.

'Follow the lane up. Photograph it all the way. Then photograph it from the body all the way down to the street,' Blades told Peacock.

'Yes, sir,' Peacock said.

Blades watched the police surgeon at work. He and Parker had not yet spoken. Then Parker grunted as he seemed to reach some conclusion. 'She's been here a few hours, this one,' he said.

'It's surprising nobody came across her before they did,' Blades said, 'though I don't expect many people go up and down this lane in the middle of the night.'

Parker continued to study the corpse. He tested for internal temperature and felt the limbs for stiffness. He made a careful inspection of the stab wounds. He collected a sample of blood. He tutted a bit, wrote notes, tutted a bit more, then sighed and stood up. 'I'll arrange to have the body taken away for a post-mortem. You'll want the time of death. I don't know. Maybe between one and two in the morning? And, initially, I see no sign of interference.'

'Was she murdered by a man or a woman?'

'There's an awfully good question, and it's hard to say. The blade has been stabbed in with force, but a woman could manage to inflict wounds like these too.'

'That's what I thought.'

'No signs of violence apart from the knife wounds. She must have been taken by surprise. There's nothing useful under the fingernails.'

'So, it could be someone she knew and trusted.'

'From my point of view, but you're the detective. Do you know who she is?'

'Oh, yes. Her bag's not here and there's no identification on the body, but if the murderer took the bag to delay our identification of the body, he was wasting his time.'

'You know who she is?'

'I interviewed her yesterday. This is someone who worked in the same shop as Daphne, they were friends at one time. Her name is Jane Proudfoot, and our suspect probably knew both of them.'

'The murderer took her bag?'

'Unless she wasn't carrying one.'

'You wouldn't think that likely.'

'Someone she knew robbed her?' Peacock said.

'I wonder if she was worth robbing,' Blades said. 'These are not expensive clothes, and that's a glass necklace she's wearing, and the killer left that.'

'Someone else could have come along later and taken the bag,' Peacock said. 'If she died between one and two as Dr Parker has said, she was lying here for a few hours.'

'If someone did that, it would be useful to trace them. They might have seen the killer.'

'I'd better be off,' Parker said. 'Any progress on the young woman on the beach?'

'We don't know who did it,' Blades replied, 'though there is one line of inquiry that might be interesting.'

'Do you think he did this?' Parker asked.

'We'll question him. He must have known both victims.'

'I hope you get him.'

As he turned to go, Blades and Peacock did the same, though Blades did leave two constables to guard the crime scene. He wasn't finished with that. As they were leaving the lane, a man approached them who wore a broad felt hat and distinctive overcoat that Blades could not fail to recognize, a tall man who seemed to loom, as he came out of the shadows. Blades' initial apprehension turned to irritation, as it always did when he met John Musgrave, a reporter for the *Birtleby Times*.

'Another body?' John's voice boomed. 'Is it another young woman?'

Blades gave thought to what statement he ought to be making at this point. He decided meeting John straight after the discovery of the body could be useful, but the first reply Blades gave was brief, as he gave consideration to what information he ought to release. 'It is.'

'Murdered in the same way?'

'I can't give details at the moment and I can't give identification either until her family has been informed. I can tell you, she was about the same age as the other victims.'

'Do you think it's the same killer?'

Blades frowned. Reporters. How could a policeman give conclusions before investigating the crime?

'I can't rule it out, but we will be exploring other possibilities as well.'

'Do you know when she was killed?'

'Sometime last night.'

'In the Khyber Pass?'

'That's right. A lurid name. And now a lurid crime has happened in it, unfortunately. It would be useful to know if anyone spotted something suspicious in the vicinity, particularly at about one or two in the morning. We need to catch this killer. We don't want this happening to another young woman.'

'Have you made progress with the murder of Daphne Tanner?'

'We are pursuing inquiries, but it would prejudice them to release details.'

'You have a suspect, then?'

Blades thought that a question to be avoided and did so. 'No one has been arrested. If that should happen, I will let you know.'

'What our readers want to know is this: is the Ridges murderer back?'

Blades pondered his reply. 'We don't even know if all of the Ridges murders were committed by the same person. It seems unlikely when the sailor Pulteney was hanged for two of them.'

'The conclusion the public came to at the time was that you'd hanged the wrong man.'

'You mean the conclusion the press came to – and there was no proof of it.'

'Is there any chance of a link between this murder and that of Daphne Tanner?'

'There's no proof of that either, though it is a line of inquiry. If we could establish links between those who knew the victims, that would help, as would links between people seen at the time at both murder scenes. Another avenue we're pursuing is that there could be a link with the murder of Elspeth Summers. We have records of witnesses who came forward at the time of that murder, but any others would be useful. We do especially appeal for witnesses to this crime. Someone probably does know who did this, even if they're not aware of it. They may have seen something suspicious in someone's behaviour. They may have noticed unexplained blood on someone's clothing. If anyone is afraid to come forward, they may rest assured we will protect them.'

Blades ended the interview there. The reporter had copy and Blades had made his plea. Perhaps both of their interests had been served.

CHAPTER TWELVE

The place where Jane had lived – which was her parents' house – looked substantial from a distance, being a large stone cottage, but, with more than one front door and several lines of washing, it was obvious on closer approach that it was split into more than one dwelling. It was Martha herself, Jane's mother, who answered the door; an alarmed look appeared on her face as soon as Blades showed his card.

'Has something happened?' she asked.

Blades didn't want the interview to take place in such a public place as a doorway, so he didn't answer the question. Instead, after a moment's pause, he asked, in the gentlest tone he could manage, 'Is it all right if we come in?' which perturbed Martha even more.

She answered her own question. 'Something has. It's Jane, isn't it?'

'It would be easier if we came in,' Blades said.

Martha took a deep breath and put her hand on the doorway as if to support herself, then turned. 'Come on in,' she said. Then she stopped and turned again. 'It's not John, is it? His boat hasn't gone down? Whenever it blows up and he's out at sea, I worry myself half to death. But it hasn't been stormy so, it can't be John, can it?'

Blades was trying to work out the best way to reply, when Martha rescued him by ushering them inside. Blades could see how cramped the Proudfoot's quarters were, though they were well enough furnished with mahogany pieces that might have seen better days but had been built to last. Two wally dugs stared at them from the fireplace. Above them, a delft black-and-white china plate urged them to think of their sins, which Blades duly did.

'Have a seat,' Martha said as she heaved herself into an armchair and waved an arm in the direction of a couch, but Blades and Peacock remained standing. This was no social call.

'I'm sorry,' Blades said. 'I didn't want to tell you outside.'

'I knew it. I knew it.' Martha put her hands to her face, which was collapsing into a mass of folds and lines. Blades struggled for the words. He could imagine Jean in this situation, and how it would affect her if anything happened to their son. 'Tell me,' Martha said.

Blades could see Peacock was starting to look at him with impatience.

'We have no news of your husband,' Blades said. 'We've no reason to suppose anything has happened to him. I'm sorry, but this is about your daughter, Jane.'

'She's dead?' Martha said.

'I'm afraid so,' Blades said. 'I'm sorry.'

'Oh no. You can't mean it? Dead?' Martha was obviously shocked and struggling to take this in. She continued talking for what seemed the sake of it. 'I'd hoped and hoped she was staying the night with Alice. And she's dead? She doesn't always tell me beforehand she's visiting her. And I thought she must be there. But it's what I wanted to think, isn't it? How did it happen? I always told Jane to be careful. And she was. She was a good girl was Jane. How did it happen?'

'We don't know the circumstances,' Blades said, 'but her body was found early this morning in an alleyway they call the Khyber Pass. She had been stabbed at about one or two in the morning.'

'Was she raped?'

'Nothing of that sort happened to her. She wasn't beaten or sexually assaulted. The police surgeon says it would have been a quick death.'

Now Martha burst into tears. The only thing Blades could think of to say was 'I'm sorry' again. Then Martha stood up and left the room. When she returned, she had recovered some composure, but her face was so white and drawn, she looked as if she had aged about twenty years. She sat in her seat again but could not bring her eyes to meet Blades'. She wrung her hands, became aware of this, and stopped. Then she did look up at the policeman opposite her.

'Is there anybody we can ask to come and be with you?' Blades asked.

'Alice, I suppose, but she's married with two children. I'll go over and visit her. In any case, I want to break this news to her myself.'

That made sense, as far as Blades could see. 'Do you mind if we ask you some questions?' he asked.

'I can manage that,' Martha replied. 'I'm a grown woman. And I want you to catch whoever did this.'

'Can you tell me where Jane was last night?' Blades asked.

Martha did not need to give that thought. 'She was at a friend's place with a few other girls, nothing wicked. They have a sewing circle.' Martha made a strangled noise which might have been meant to be a laugh. 'How can anyone get themselves murdered at a sewing circle?' She cackled again and Blades noted the hysteria.

'Do you know where they met and what the names of the other girls were?'

Martha told Blades where Jane had been and who she had been with.

'Did Jane complain of anyone recently?'

'What do you mean?'

'Has she been receiving unwelcome attentions, or has anyone been behaving in a threatening way towards her?'

'She would have told me about that, and she didn't.'

'Did Jane have any men friends?'

'She was engaged to be married, but her young man died in the war.'

Blades sighed. Not that story again, he thought. It had happened to so many young women.

'That war destroyed a lot of lives, Jane's included. I kept telling her that John would have wanted her to meet someone else, to lead a full life, to have fun. But she never seemed interested in anyone else.' Then she paused, before continuing. 'Except that Frank Bywaters. I don't know what she saw in him. And he wasn't interested.'

'Frank Bywaters?' Blades said.

'That's the one,' Martha replied. 'A scarecrow with sticky-out ears, and the girls were fascinated with him – before he became a conchie at least.'

Daphne was for one, Blades was thinking. That made two young women – and both dead.

* * *

Blades and Peacock went around interviewing everyone who had been at that sewing circle, and the women agreed it had been a normal meeting, with everyday chatter, and the sharing of sewing tips. Blades asked if they knew about any men Jane had been seeing but they did not. There had been gossip about their own menfolk, but Jane had made no contribution to that. They said Jane had slight interest in the species, which struck Blades as odd. Jane was not a woman with no interest in men, so was there someone she was keeping secret about? If so, why, and who? Which was speculation. There could be nobody. It could be that, thwarted by Frank, she was lying fallow. What was useful was that they were told the time that Jane left, which was ten o'clock at night. At that point, her friends had bid farewell to her outside Marie Croft's cottage in Marchmount, and she had started on her walk home. All going well, that ought to have taken Jane about half an hour, yet the police surgeon reckoned she had met her end in the Khyber Pass between one and two in the morning. What had she been doing in the time in between? Blades cursed that reporter for his prompt arrival at the crime scene. If Blades had been given more time before going public, he could have asked if anyone knew where Jane had been after ten. He supposed someone might come forward to say that all the same, and an update could be given to the press later.

'Could she have been seeing Frank?' Peacock asked when they were back at the station.

Blades was standing at the stove warming his hands. He grunted, then turned to Peacock. 'In any other case, Parker has always said how difficult it is to estimate when death occurred. In this one, he instantly gives a more or less precise time. Perhaps he was right before when he said that isn't possible.'

Peacock was seated at his desk; in front of him, a pile of reports which he was ignoring. 'If time of death was between ten and eleven the body lay on a public footpath for a long time before being discovered.'

Blades' eyes held Peacock's. There was an alertness in Peacock's face, as if he were readying himself for a contest, even though it was only a sharing of minds. 'It was dark,' Blades said. 'Do people like using that passage at night? I don't think I would. It's steep. It's not lit. It would be easy to lose your footing there and hurt yourself. And it's not overlooked. Yet, it's where we found her. She might have gone there with someone.'

Peacock nodded. 'Frank? If not, it's a good spot for a random murder. She presented the opportunity, and someone took it.'

'I think there's a link to Daphne's murder,' Blades said. He reached in his pocket for a pack of cigarettes, then offered one to Peacock. 'They were in the same social circle – and they had Frank Bywaters in common, our conscientious objector with his high and mighty views of the sanctity of human life; his own at least.' Blades lit a safety match and proffered it to Peacock, who puffed at the cigarette. Blades continued speaking. 'Frank strikes me as being a self-obsessed individual. He didn't care what he put his family through by refusing to report for military duty. And he's split Daphne's family. He didn't mind estranging her from her aunt's family or her brother. Does he understand people as well as ideas?'

'Just a man of principle?' Peacock suggested.

Blades lit his own cigarette, then breathed out the smoke, but he did not appear all that interested in it. His mind was elsewhere. 'Who happens to suffer from a serious lack of empathy. He understands it as an idea. He knows how to express it when putting forward an argument for being a conscientious objector. It's just that he doesn't feel any?'

'He has feelings for Daphne.'

Blades felt his mind racing now, or was he letting his thoughts run away with him? 'As a conquest or what? Maybe he thinks he needs a wife for social standing. He comes from a conventional family – with middle-class pretensions.'

Peacock nodded. 'He also has a better chance of establishing himself in teaching again if he's married.'

Blades stabbed his cigarette at the air as he gestured with his hand. 'So, why kill her? Had she decided to finish with him? Her family don't mention it, though her brother could have been having another go at her and finally persuaded her.'

99

'Not that we know of.'

Blades began to pace as if in pursuit of his own thoughts. Then he stopped himself and turned towards Peacock again.

'Even if Frank did kill Daphne, why would he kill Jane?'

'Did she know something?'

'It's not likely. She hadn't even had much to do with Daphne lately.'

'Maybe she did and had arranged to meet with Frank to talk about what she knew.'

'If she did know something, why not tell the police?'

'Unless she wasn't quite sure of what it was she had seen?' Blades could see that Peacock was beginning to be frustrated by these arguments; he was stubbing his cigarette out, though he had smoked little of it.

'If he did kill her,' Peacock replied, 'it doesn't matter why he did it. He knows why. It might not even make sense to us. We need to concentrate on what witness statements we can conjure up.'

'All right,' Blades said. 'Let's see what information the constables turn up from people living near the Khyber Pass.'

Peacock returned his thoughts to Frank. 'As we've said, a CO might be possible, but it would be a real turn up all the same.'

It might be too surprising, Blades was thinking. 'We need to find out what his fellow COs in the Non-Combatant Corps thought of him. Did he fit in with them? Was he just looking for an easy way out of the war?'

Then, Blades sat further back in his seat. He took a deep draw of his cigarette. 'So, our Frank – mocked and derided by the actual soldiers, maybe by his fellow conchies too, just behind the line or even in it, possibly as much a candidate for shellshock as any soldier – comes back to a life he has ruined for himself by not fighting. There's no job for him with the standing that he had, and he has to scratch away part-time in a poorly-thought-of school. That's enough to make anyone bitter, and he was maybe a bit odd and intense in the first place. A person like that could have done it. Something could have gone wrong inside him. He could have done both, which is a nice theory. And we need facts to back it up. Equally, are there any that suggest he didn't commit these murders? But we won't interview Frank yet. We'll wait till witness statements start coming in.'

CHAPTER THIRTEEN

It was Robert whom Blades interviewed first as he was
their suspect for the first murder, he had a connection with
Elspeth, and he had also known Jane. Blades could see that
he was on edge as he sat in the interview room: he was
biting a thumbnail as Blades and Peacock entered. The
face he turned to them was pale, and his eyes stared with
an unusual intensity. They seated themselves opposite him.
Blades had not allowed Robert the company of his father
for this interview as, if this was their man, they needed to
see him on his own. Peacock took out his black notebook
and placed it on the table with his pencil beside it. Blades
did not speak but studied Robert, who looked up at the
window, then across to the door, then across to Blades,
before he allowed his gaze to settle on the floor.

When he spoke, Blades used a deliberately benign voice
in contrast to the forbidding look he had already aimed at
Robert. 'There are some details we need, to help us with
our investigation. You know how it is. We keep aiming at a
bigger picture.'

Robert's look at Blades was uncertain, but he nodded.
Blades took out a file from the desk drawer and leafed
through one or two pages, before addressing Robert in a

conversational tone. 'You knew Elspeth Summers, didn't you?'

Robert gave an intake of breath. 'Elspeth? That was some time ago. Why are you asking me about her?'

Blades fell back on Peacock's phrase. 'Background information,' he said. 'You'd be surprised how much of that we need to collect. You don't mind, do you?'

There was a blank look on Robert's face. 'Don't mind?' he said. An irate look took over. 'Will it make any difference if I do?' Blades noticed Robert's hand had tightened into a fist.

'You used to drink in the Victoria when she worked there as a barmaid?' Blades said.

'So did a lot of other people. What if I did?'

'Did you get on with her?'

'I ordered drinks from her. She served them up. I paid her.'

'Not much room for argument there,' Blades said.

'No.' Robert did not elaborate.

'What did you think of her?'

'I don't know. She was pretty, I suppose.'

'You liked her?'

'I didn't know her. She seemed all right. I feel a bit of sympathy for barmaids, if it matters. It must be difficult dealing with some of the men they get in there.'

'So, you thought you'd have a pleasant chat with her?'

Robert stared back at Blades, who noticed Robert had started drumming his fingers now. Then Robert said something under his breath which Blades supposed he had not intended him to catch. A dubious silence fell as Robert stared at the desk. Peacock continued compiling notes in his clear, steady hand.

'A chat is hardly illegal,' Blades said to Robert.

Robert's eyes flashed their irritation directly at Blades. 'Beyond ordering drinks, I didn't say anything to Elspeth.'

'But you did speak to your sister, I suppose?'

103

Robert's eyes flared again. 'What's that supposed to mean?'

'Were you getting on with your sister latterly?'

'We always got on. It was easy to get on with Daphne. She was a good kid.'

'Didn't it annoy you when she became engaged to Frank Bywaters?'

'She made up her own mind about things and you had to respect it.'

Now it was Blades who started drumming his fingers. He was not getting anywhere here. Robert gave Blades an insolent stare.

'You said that you walked off by yourself after that quarrel you had with Helen,' Blades said.

'You've asked that before and I answered you.'

'When you said you didn't go anywhere near the Ridges?'

A look of what seemed like realisation appeared on Robert's face. He gave thought to his reply, then said, 'I didn't.'

Blades kept his voice neutral and let the words speak for themselves. 'We have a witness who says they saw you walking along the Ridges at that time.'

Robert shifted in his seat. Blades saw that his lips had tightened, and he was now in something approaching fury.

'I deny it.'

Blades kept his questioning calm. 'Let's suppose you did. After a huge argument with your girlfriend when she finished with you, you walked along the Ridges to cool off. Where you came across your sister.'

'It didn't happen,' Robert replied.

'Whom you'd had so many arguments with about Frank Bywaters.'

Robert snorted.

'You've admitted to that in a previous interview,' Blades said.

'One or two heated discussions and that's all. Frank Bywaters was a stigma for the whole family.'

'If you say so, sir.' Was Robert biting his lip now? It looked as if he was. 'Did you blame her for the fact Helen finished with you?'

'No.'

Robert was frustrating, as his answers did not convey much. Blades supposed he should continue to try to pressure him.

'The problem was, Helen didn't want to marry into a family with a conscientious objector?'

'If you say so. I didn't.'

'You were in a tizzy already when you met up with Daphne on the Ridges. Did you tell her that Helen had finished with you? Did Daphne say something about that you did not like? Some people might have lashed out in a fury, without thinking about what they were doing.'

'That's a good story you're making up. And that's what it is.'

'We do know about your temper, Mr Tanner.'

'What temper?' Robert said, but Blades did notice that Robert twisted about on his seat. 'This is garbage,' Robert said. 'I don't know why I'm having to listen to this.' Then he stood up and Blades and Peacock wondered what he was about to do. Robert put his face close to Blades and hissed at him. 'You've no right to make accusations like that. They're rubbish.' Blades noticed that Peacock's pencil was now flat on the table and both hands were free. Robert noticed this too.

'Sit down and calm yourself,' Blades said. 'Anger won't help.'

'It just proves you have a temper,' Peacock said.

Robert glared at Peacock. He opened his mouth to say something but closed it again. Then he did sit down. Blades said nothing as he waited for Robert to regain some calmness. Then Blades began speaking again.

'How did you get on with Jane Proudfoot?'

The question disturbed any composure Robert might have found, and he replied with an increased intensity. 'Yes, I heard about her murder. You're asking me about that too? I don't believe this. I'm a man who's done nothing, and here I am, being accused of the murder of three women? You ought to be sacked. First, there was that debacle of the Ridges when you hanged the wrong man, and, not satisfied with that, you want to do it again.'

No, Blades thought. That case was not going to bury itself, and he was the one feeling uncomfortable now.

'Where were you on the night of Monday 27th August?'

'Is that when Jane died?'

Blades nodded but, again, Robert did not answer. 'Look, I liked Jane. She was OK. A bit opinionated but who isn't? She used to be a friend of Daphne's and she would come around to the house with her, but Daphne didn't keep up with her and that stopped. I haven't seen her since.'

'You can't tell us where you were?' Blades asked.

Robert glared again. 'If you insist. I was at the Victoria with friends in the early part of the evening but went home early – about eight. I didn't leave the house after that.'

'Which your parents will verify?'

'Yes.'

Blades gave this some thought. 'You knew three women who have all turned up dead. You do understand you're bound to be questioned about that.'

'You've been doing more than asking questions. You've been accusing me of this and you've no right. A lot of other people knew all three of them. Birtleby is a small town. Why don't you have all of them in and ask them questions?'

'We will do. We will find this killer.'

'And the sooner the better, so you can leave me alone.'

As, in his opinion, he had gained from Robert what he was going to for now, Blades closed the interview. He was aware that, if it had been some kind of contest, he had not won it. But that alibi would be checked.

* * *

There was a missing murder weapon – a knife – and whoever had committed the murder must have blood on their clothes. It was time Robert's house was searched. When Blades and Peacock, with uniformed policemen in tow, turned up at the Tanners' with their search warrant, Marion and Pete were horrified.

'Have you no sense of decorum?' Pete snapped at them. 'We've just lost our daughter. Have you no respect for our feelings?'

'You can't think that any of us would have done such a thing?' Marion pleaded. She cast anxious eyes about as Blades and Peacock and two burly constables entered the cottage.

'It's just our elimination process,' Blades said as he asked the way to Robert's room. He and Peacock would search that.

'It's no such thing,' Pete said, 'but, as you're insisting on doing this, I'll show you.'

'If you just tell us where it is, sir?' Blades said. 'It will make things easier for us if you stay down here.'

Pete directed them, and Blades and Peacock strode up the hallway towards the back of the cottage. Pete called after them. 'Robert's done nothing. You ought to be out looking for the man who did this, not bothering Robert. He gave his right arm for this country.'

Blades stopped and turned round. 'If your son is innocent, he has nothing to worry about, because that's what we'll establish. I do realise this is difficult, but you will make it easier on yourself if you don't interfere.'

Pete opened his mouth as if to say something, an exasperated look still on his face, but he changed his mind. Blades continued to Robert's room.

It was small, not much bigger than a cupboard, and Blades wondered if that was what it had originally been, but Robert was lucky to have somewhere of his own. Blades noticed the untidiness of the room, with unwashed clothing lying in a pile on the floor in a corner. Blades sorted through them looking for signs of blood but did not see any. He would have the central lab look at them in any case. Then he strode to the window as a thought came into his mind, and, yes, there on the back green was something that did interest him: flapping in the breeze from a rope stretched across, family washing, with male shirts and trousers. If Robert had the sense, anything he had been wearing that night would already have been washed.

Blades sent a constable down to gather that evidence together, while Blades and Peacock continued their search of the room, attempting not to get in each other's way in the limited space. They opened the dresser drawers and turned through the clothing there, then took the drawers out and searched behind and under them but found nothing incriminating there. The bed was stripped and examined. Peacock crawled right underneath it but unearthed only a spider's web. They scrutinised the floorboards. Blades pressed down with his foot in different places, as he searched for any unusual give that might signify a hiding place. The walls held no pictures that could have anything hidden behind or in them, and the curtains contained no secret folds. There was no murder weapon in this room, not that Blades ever expected things to be simple. He swept his eyes around. What was most noticeable was the lack of anything worthy of attention. Did Robert keep no private things? The most personal item in the room had been the service medals they had found at the back of the drawer containing Robert's socks, and that box had a neglected look: if it had ever been opened, that had been but once. What did all this suggest? Someone with a lack of interest in things? Someone who had given up on life? There was an emptiness here. What might Robert be driven to in order to fill that?

There was no sign of excitement on the faces of the constables they had left searching the rest of the cottage. Constable Flockhart ventured his report. 'Nothing incriminating. There is a kitchen with the usual range of kitchen knives in it, but none with blood on them.'

Blades glanced across at them. They would be sent to the central lab too. Blades' eyes were drawn to the basket with clothes brought in from the washing line ready for the iron, and he leafed through the items there, stopping to look at a cuff. He picked it up and showed it to Peacock.

'What does that look like?'

Peacock gazed at it. 'As if someone has been washing blood off and left a spot.'

'Faded, but blood?'

'Yes.'

'We'll have that tested.' He turned to Marion. 'There was blood on this?' he said.

Marion stared at it, a frightened look on her face. Then, words burst out of her. 'What of it? There was, yes. And I do my best to be a good housewife, so I cleaned it with the rest. There's nothing wrong with that.'

'Whose shirt is it?' Blades asked.

Pete replied. 'It's Robert's. He cut himself chopping sticks. That's a difficult job for someone with one arm. The axe bounced back on him. I tell him not to do that chore, to leave it to me, but he likes to prove he can still do the things he did before. I can't stop him.'

Pete looked across at Marion for support and she nodded. Blades wondered at the truth of it. It was something else to ask Robert about. He turned to the basket and picked through the other items again. 'We'll have this all bagged and checked.'

Then he turned to Flockhart. 'Did you search the wash-house?'

'We've been busy in here,' Flockhart replied.

'And keep at it. In fact, search everywhere twice. Every cupboard. All the rubbish bins. And have a good look at those floorboards. Could anything be hidden under those?'

'Yes, sir.'

Doing his best to avoid looking at Pete and Marion, Blades opened the back door and strode out, followed by Peacock. The wash-house was at the bottom of the green, and much like any other, a brick building with tiny casement windows. Blades opened the door and stepped into a bare room with its stone floor and its copper and mangle. Blades studied the floor for signs of blood but saw none. It had been recently washed, which might be the reason. The sink was spotless too. He opened the cupboard under it. There was soap, but there were no knives and no bloody clothes. He pulled himself straight again, gave the wash-house a withering look and strode out.

CHAPTER FOURTEEN

The tramp Blades' constables brought into the station was an unwilling, cursing ferment of flailing limbs and words as he stood in front of the police sergeant's desk. Sergeant Ryan noticed that the constables had stood well back from their prisoner, so he could thrust his fists impotently at thin air. Constable Flockhart gave Sergeant Ryan a weary look. The tramp glared at Sergeant Ryan from an untidy head with a three-day beard on it and locks that had not made the acquaintance of a barber in some time. His faded clothes displayed inexpertly sewn patches, and a torn trouser leg showed a sickly white kneecap. The stench of alcohol coming from him was pungent. Sergeant Ryan moved back from his desk. He attempted to muster patience but failed. The bark he aimed at the man was brusque.

'What mayhem have you been causing now, Jed?' It was not the first time that Sergeant Ryan had met this particular tramp.

'I was minding my own business, when your overgrown constables grabbed hold of me.' Jed spoke his words with rapidity as if there could be a lot more to come.

Flockhart interrupted the impassioned flow. 'He was having a fist fight with another man when we came across him.'

'Not minding your own business, Jed,' Ryan said.

'It was my own business. That man attacked me, and I needed to defend myself.'

Sergeant Ryan glanced at the other man, standing quietly behind the constables. 'Is this the man you were fighting with, Jed?'

'He's not a man. He's a stinking rat,' Jed said.

The man grimaced but said nothing.

'We had to drag Jed off this young man before he did him serious and permanent damage,' Flockhart said.

The other constable nodded his head.

'And what's your name, sir?' the sergeant asked the man.

'Mark Enright.'

'You're from Birtleby, are you, sir?'

'I'm from Leeds. I'm down here to visit my aunt.'

'So, what happened, sir?'

'I was walking past a bench on the seafront when I was set upon.'

Jed's querulous voice piped up again. 'You were after my bottle.'

'I wasn't after your filthy bottle.'

'It might be hard to believe, Jed, but not everybody has the fascination for cheap spirits that you have,' Ryan said.

'I could see what he was about. He was sneaking up on it.'

'I wasn't,' the young man replied.

'What day of the week is it, Jed?' Ryan asked him.

Jed's reply was immediate. 'Wednesday. What kind of question is that? I know which day of the week it is.'

'Only two days out,' Ryan replied. 'Not bad.'

'What do you mean? Two days out?'

'It's Friday,' Jed's victim said.

'See. He knows his onions,' Ryan said.

112

Jed's face had a flabbergasted expression on it. 'You're making this up.'

'All that cheap whisky's going for your brain,' Ryan said.

'Has addled it,' Flockhart corrected.

'What does it matter which day of the week it is?' pouted Jed. 'That doesn't change anything. He assaulted me and you're tormenting an innocent man who was only trying to protect his bottle.'

'What's the reason for bringing them in?' Ryan asked Flockhart.

'The protection of the public – from Jed, that is, not Mr Enright.' Flockhart continued, 'My attention was called to a commotion along the front, at which point I blew my whistle and was in time joined by Constable Banks. Two men were brawling. Mr Enright was attempting to protect himself from a determined attack by Jed, and I went over to them and subdued Jed. He offered to take me on as well. Mr Enright stood to one side and apologised to me.'

Sergeant Ryan nodded to the two constables. 'Lead the two men into the interview room and take their statements. We'll charge Jed with drunken affray.'

Jed glowered and pulled himself up to his full height. 'I'm as sober as the day I was born. Drunken affray! That's rubbish.' He swayed as he continued. 'It's those constables who ought to be charged. They assaulted me.'

'We will take your point of view into account, Jed, before we ignore it,' Ryan said.

'You're not really going to charge me?' The indignation in Jed's voice was sincere, but there was a self-pitying look on his face now, instead of angry bluster.

'It is a pity to dirty a clean cell,' Ryan replied, 'but there you are.'

'But I can be helpful to you. I know things.'

Ryan gave him a disbelieving look. 'Do you remember your name?'

'What kind of question's that? Of course I do, and lots of other things. Don't you want to solve that case?'

Sergeant Ryan gave him a querying look, but the tone in his voice suggested he was humouring Jed when he said, 'Which case?'

'The murder of that young woman on the beach.'

'The murder of–' Ryan paused. 'What could you know about that?' he asked.

'You might be surprised. Do you want me to tell you or not?'

Ryan stared at Jed. 'So, tell us,' he said.

'Only if you'll drop that trumped up charge,' he said.

'Not a chance,' Ryan said.

'Then I won't tell,' Jed said.

'I doubt if you know anything,' Ryan said. 'We're not interested in statements witnesses have just made up.'

'You know how to insult a man, don't you?' Jed said. 'But you don't know who did that murder. I do.'

Flockhart spoke up now. 'Go on, Jed. Give us all a laugh. Tell us.'

'I've a good mind not to,' Jed said, 'after a remark like that from a whippersnapper like you. Whippersnapper. Whippersnapper.' His eyes bored into Flockhart.

Flockhart shrugged. Ryan turned to him. 'Take them through to the witness room and take statements. Then we'll lock Jed up.'

'All right, as you're so keen, I'll tell you,' Jed said.

But Ryan was no longer listening. His mind had turned to the job of cleaning up the cell after Jed had been in it. Did they have delousing powder?

'I was just minding my own business,' Jed was saying.

'Again,' Ryan said, but he had already turned away from him. Flockhart reached for Jed's arm to lead him through to the interview room.

'You'd never have thought a one-armed man could have done that, would you?' Jed said.

Now he did have the attention of Sergeant Ryan and Constables Flockhart and Banks. Ryan knew all about that case, and he knew about Daphne's one-armed brother, as did the constables. Ryan gave Jed a good hard look. A picture had come into his mind of the swaying Jed on a witness stand and the impression he would make on a jury. Even if Jed had seen something, Ryan was not sure how much help it would be. All the same, his statement ought to be taken. If it amounted to anything, it could be reported to Inspector Blades.

'Continue taking him through,' Ryan said to Flockhart. 'Listen to what Jed has to say about the one-armed man and take a statement. Leave Mr Enright here.'

'Right you are, Sarge,' Flockhart said, and he and Constable Banks led Jed through to the interview room.

'I wasn't doing anything to him when he set on me,' Enright said to Ryan, who listened respectfully. This young man was a different kettle of fish. His trousers weren't held up with string, for a start. He wore a suit, which if inexpensive looking, was newish and smart. He had his hat in his hands, and couldn't stop fiddling with it. It was a broad-brimmed felt hat of a fashionable type.

'When my constables came across you, they say you were in the middle of a fist fight with Jed Wilkinson.'

'I'm allowed to defend myself, I hope. That's all I was doing.'

'A reasonable self-defence is allowed, yes,' Ryan replied, and there was an understanding tone in his voice. 'How did the fight start, sir?'

'I was walking along the Shore Road. That's an innocent enough thing to do.'

'Of course, sir, and what happened?'

'What's that man's name again? You said it was Jed.' Ryan nodded. 'Well, Jed was begging. He had a tray of pencils he was trying to sell. He was swaying about all over the place. I definitely didn't want to buy one. He'd let off a dreadful stream of invective to the last person he'd been trying to sell to when they refused to buy one, which was when I decided to cross the road. Jed shouted at me before I'd got more than a step or two across, and I turned and told him he was on a respectable street and he ought to behave better than that. I wish I hadn't. I wish I'd ignored him. Anyway, he harangued me, told me he was a wounded soldier. He'd fought to keep his country safe. What right did I have to cross the road to avoid talking to him?'

'There was nothing said about a bottle, then, sir?'

'Nothing at all. He's made that up.'

'Do you know anything about this one-armed man he was talking about?'

'Not a thing. I wouldn't believe any of that. It's another story. A way of getting out of trouble. You should just lock him up.'

'He annoyed you, sir?'

'He pummelled me with his fists. That is annoying.'

'You were telling me about how the fight started, sir. I still haven't quite got that.'

'He was haranguing me. So, I told him what I thought of him for ranting at innocent passers-by while he stood there swaying away. I was wasting my time saying anything to him. I should have walked on by.' He paused, his fingers still kneading the rim of his hat, before continuing, 'Then, the man started going on about all his bad luck, the poor family he'd come from, and any chance he'd had in life had been taken away from him by that war. Then he held up his tray of pencils and said, "Help a hero, sir." I shouldn't have let that annoy me, but when I thought of some of the men I fought beside, it did. I doubted if he was even there, a snivelling wretch like him. I told him that too. Tore him off quite a strip, which I know I shouldn't have done. That's when he put the tray to one side and attacked me. He struck the first blow, and the second, then the third and I just had to step back and try to wallop him too. But I'd no choice. As I say, I have the right to defend myself.'

'And if that's all verified, you have nothing to worry about, sir. There were others there?'

'Oh, yes, and the constables questioned them. It should all hold up.'

Sergeant Ryan looked at the man, who still had a worried look on his face as he was sure he was in trouble over this altercation as well.

'I'll just take your statement, sir.'

* * *

Blades and Peacock were still seated in the interview room after questioning Jed. Blades was in a quandary. Jed Wilkinson's statement did bear out the other witness account that put Robert firmly at the Ridges at the time of the murder, but neither witness would present a plausible figure in court.

'Should we be showing bias against gentlemen of the road?' Peacock asked.

'I'm not, but a jury will.'

'The war shipwrecked a lot of men. You see old soldiers selling boot laces and the like everywhere. The work's not there or they're damaged, and employers won't take them on.'

'Which only adds to my argument.' Blades paused as he wished that it did not. 'A jury will look twice at them too.'

'But if Robert is our man, we need to have him behind bars before he kills someone else.'

'We think it's Robert?' Blades asked.

'He's bitter enough. He was destroyed by the war.'

Blades nodded. 'If he snapped, someone like that might be capable of anything. And he does fly into tempers. We know that from Helen. She says he's hit her before, and she's terrified of him. That day she'd finished with him and he stormed off. It would be easy to imagine the scenario we have for him: walking along the beach, coming across Daphne, arguing with her, then lashing out.'

'He denies being on the Ridges.'

'Because he'll be accused of the murder if he admits to that. We need to prove he was there – and we probably do need more than we have, frustrating as that is.'

'Did he kill Jane Proudfoot as well? We have a shirt with bloodstains on it.'

'But then, there's the alibi.'

'He was at his parents' house. Could he have sneaked out?'

Blades tapped his finger on the desk. 'We can ask them.'

'We need the layout of his parents' cottage,' Peacock said, 'and we have to establish where Robert is supposed to have been in the house. We don't have to take their word for it.'

'What would really help,' Blades said, 'is if a witness could place him outside the house when his parents thought he was inside. Then that's him linked with two murders.'

'All we have to do is assemble proof.'

Blades drummed his finger again. 'I wonder if we can tie him into Elspeth's death properly?'

'Could we arrange another newspaper report?'

'And if we make Robert think the evidence is conclusive, he might even break down and confess.'

'If we give the *Birtleby Times* another smidgeon or two of information, they'll jump at the chance of another article.'

The two policemen looked at each other. They seemed to have things worked out. Did they?

CHAPTER FIFTEEN

*A link has been suggested between the murders of
Daphne Tanner on the Ridges and Jane Proudfoot in
Birtleby's Khyber Pass. Inspector Blades of North
Yorkshire Constabulary states that, though the
murders were committed in different ways, Daphne
Tanner being hit with a blunt object, and Jane
Proudfoot being stabbed to death, a connection between
the two women does suggest the same murderer. Both
worked in the same millinery store in the Town
Square, Hargreaves' Millinery. Police appeal for
witnesses to the two murders. Daphne was killed on
the afternoon of Tuesday 21st August on the Ridges.
Jane died at some time on Monday night, the 27th
August in the Khyber Pass. If anyone has information
about any person or persons they saw near either of
these places at these times, they should get in touch
with Birtleby Police Station. The police would also
like to know if there was someone in the young
women's circle of friends who had a grudge against*

them. If anyone knows anything about this, please come forward. This newspaper continues to express its sympathy with the family and friends of both girls at this difficult time.

After the article appeared, Blades and Peacock did not have long to wait for responses. One demure, elderly lady gave a shocked account of a tramp who, as described, had an unerring similarity to Jed. She said that he had been strolling along the sea-front on the afternoon of Daphne's murder. Though she had to admit she had seen nothing of Daphne or her dog when he was there, she had noticed the vagrant wandering aimlessly as he cursed to himself and at anyone who came near him. She supposed he was trying to beg, but thought he was far too aggressive to have much success. He seemed the worse for drink and it would not surprise her if he had murdered somebody.

One of our witnesses, Blades thought. If the defence lawyer got hold of this old lady, he could tear Jed to bits on the witness stand. Blades even considered whether Jed might be the sinister tramp described as such by his fellow gents of the road.

One witness gave an account of a mystery car hovering in the neighbourhood. A man in it had offered lifts to young ladies. The date of the sighting was different, and it took place in a different area of Birtleby, so it seemed to have nothing to do with this case. Still, it would be followed up.

Someone else claimed to have seen a sailor quarrelling with a young woman on the Ridges, which reminded Blades of a similar statement at the time of one of the Ridges murders. This witness could give no convincing description of either the sailor or the young woman, and Blades thought this probably an irrelevant account, though it would be borne in mind.

Then a young man of respectable appearance, and who was employed at the same firm where Robert had worked, turned up and placed Robert on the Ridges at about the time of Daphne's murder. This seemed to be a breakthrough, though Blades did not accept any account at face value. This young man admitted he had a history of arguments with Robert, which had something to do with the fact that, unlike Robert, he had not fought in the war. When he was called up, he was declared unfit. What Robert resented was not only that this young man did not have to endure trench life, but that he remained healthy enough for his normal peacetime work – and as a tailor, the job Robert could no longer do. Still, this young man was respectable and would look good on a witness stand. Would the number of witnesses they had now assembled be enough to present a case?

No witnesses placed anyone near Jane's murder, and nothing turned up to link Robert with it, which made Blades feel despondent. Perhaps there would be no break in that case. Just as he had decided that, a witness did turn up, saying that they had seen Frank Bywaters near the Khyber Pass that night. That surprised Blades and Peacock. A link between Frank Bywaters and Jane Proudfoot was firming up. Jane could have met up with a young man that night. Why could it not have been Frank? They knew Jane had been attracted to him and quarrelled with Daphne over him. They needed to make inquiries, at least.

The case against Robert for killing Jane was still weak. The blood-stained shirt was not enough by itself. The case against him for the murder of Daphne was improving. Three witnesses placed him near the scene, and the psychology was there, which gave opportunity and motive, and the means was there in the shape of any number of rocks on the beach that could be wielded. They could bring him in and see what transpired when they told him of the evidence mounting against him. Blades knew a confession was always possible. Then they would have the murderer of Daphne Tanner.

* * *

As he sat in the interview room opposite Blades and Peacock again, Robert looked a picture of concentrated fury, his body tense, the muscles in his face taut, and his eyes boring into Blades. His silence seemed to give greater expression to his feelings than any words might. When they had arrived at his house to ask him to come in for questioning, Robert had said more than enough; he had put across his self-righteous anger fluently. He only agreed to accompany them when it was explained to him that there were sufficient grounds to arrest him. Robert's father had told him to insist on having a lawyer present, but Blades had said it was only a matter of assisting with inquiries at the moment, and Robert had gone along with that, saying only a guilty man would need one, and that lawyers were an absurd expense. He told his father he would be released after about five minutes. Pete Tanner had not looked convinced but had acceded to Robert's judgement.

Blades felt in no hurry to begin the interview. The more on edge Robert was, the more careless he might be with his answers. Peacock made his usual pantomime of taking out his black notebook, opening it, flattening the page, taking out a pencil, sharpening it, and then placing it on the desk beside the book. Blades tapped a finger firmly twice, then began.

'These are no longer background inquiries.' He studied Robert's reaction. Robert's hand clenched into a fist. 'There are grounds to suppose you were on the Ridges at the time of your sister's murder.' Robert's lips tightened and his eyes burned into Blades. 'We have three different witnesses who place you there.' Robert muttered something indecipherable, shifted in his seat, then turned his head to glare out of the window at the brick wall opposite. 'Which is a weight of evidence, sir. You were there.'

Robert turned back to face Blades. 'Not on the Ridges, I wasn't.' Robert's face now held a deflated look, but the anger was no less. 'All right. We did meet each other on the front, but I didn't go anywhere near the Ridges.'

Peacock tutted disbelievingly as he wrote down the reply Robert had made. Robert glowered at Peacock before directing a brief, conciliatory smile towards Blades.

'We came across each other,' Robert said. 'She did go along in the direction of the Ridges when she left me – after the dog. Maybe I should have stopped her. I don't know. I was thinking of something else, the row I'd just had with Helen. It had been a while since the Ridges murders and everyone thought that maniac had gone away – to America some said, where he was caught for another murder over there. I wish I had followed my sister or gone after the dog instead of her. It's supposed to be my job to take Pooky out. How do you think I feel about things? I wish I had.' Then the words stopped, and Robert stared at the now limp, flat hand he held on the table in front of him.

'What did you say to each other?' Blades asked.

'Let's see. Hello? What are you doing along here? She wondered why I had such an unhappy face and I told her. She said she was sorry. Did I want to walk along with her and Pooky? I said I wanted to be on my own for a while – thinking of myself as usual, as people tell me I do. She said it was alright, that she understood. Then we parted and walked off in different directions – unfortunately.'

Robert's face was now an agony of anxiety, and his eyes flitted everywhere but in the direction of Blades or Peacock. Blades considered what Robert had said.

'Did you see anyone else?'

'I didn't notice anybody. I was upset. I wasn't paying attention to anything. I might not have noticed Daphne when I did if she hadn't spoken to me.'

Blades continued to consider Robert. He was succeeding in presenting himself as an innocent, misunderstood man, but was it an act? Could Robert put on such a successful pretence? So many suspects could, Blades supposed, so why not Robert? Then again, what exactly had the witnesses seen? They'd testified to seeing Robert on the Ridges. They hadn't seen him with Daphne, but they had seen him walking in the direction she had gone. Supposing that to be true, and Robert's denial of being on the Ridges to be false, things could still have transpired as Robert said, just not where he said. But, Blades thought, it did all add up. It did look as if Robert had done it.

Blades decided it was time to question Robert about Jane's murder. 'Can you explain how blood came to be on one of your shirts?' he said.

'Blood? Mother did say you'd mentioned a shirt.'

'The shirt had been washed but not well enough, and we did establish the blood on it was human.'

A look of defiance appeared on Robert's face. 'I cut myself when I was chopping wood.' He pointed to the empty sleeve. 'Some things are awkward.'

'When did you cut yourself?'

Robert told him.

'On the same day that Jane Proudfoot was murdered you cut yourself when chopping wood?'

Robert's stare at Blades held anger. 'I didn't murder Jane. That's ridiculous.'

'Nobody is accusing you of anything, sir. We're asking questions and trying to establish what did happen in certain situations.'

'Oh, yes, that's all.' Robert snorted.

'We have examined your parents' house. Looking at the positions of the rooms, it would have been possible for you to creep out of the house without them knowing on the night of Jane's murder.'

Indignation blazed from Robert's eyes as he said, 'You've no witnesses who saw me doing that.'

Blades returned Robert's look with deliberate calmness.

'Not yet,' he replied.

'And I'm quite sure you have to do more than just prove that it was possible.'

Blades tapped his finger again.

CHAPTER SIXTEEN

Chief Constable Moffat's room was designed to make an impression on a visitor, from the polished floor to Moffat's grandiose oak desk with its well-padded, leather-upholstered captain's style chair – a distinct contrast to the one Blades now found himself seated in with its hard seat and upright back. Blades never enjoyed sitting there, particularly now, when it was the result of a summons. Moffat wanted to know what progress, if any, he was making. The frown on Moffat's face as he asked that question always made Blades feel it would be a very good idea to be ready to charge someone with something.

'So, who's your main suspect?' Moffat asked.

'The brother of the victim, Robert Tanner. We have three witnesses who place him at the approach to Daphne's murder scene at about the time the murder was committed. There is evidence he was in a highly emotionally charged state, and that there had been a series of arguments between him and his sister. He admits being on the shore and meeting his sister but denies being on the Ridges, probably a lie. There is evidence as to his character. He is a generally disturbed, angry and violent individual who beat his fiancé, which is why she finished with him. As a man, he has been destroyed by the war. He lost an arm, his trade, and his stability.'

'So, we can place him there,' Moffat said. 'He had the means. It's easy enough to pick up a rock with one arm. He has the personality type, which gives sufficient motive. All that gives grounds for charging him.'

'We were continuing to look for proof before going that far.'

'More proof would always be better,' Moffat said.

Blades studied him. This was a man who wanted results by yesterday, which did not allow much room for second thoughts.

'But there isn't any point in pussyfooting about,' Moffat continued. He did think Blades too hesitant after the apparent debacle over Pulteney. He'd even questioned whether Blades had lost his nerve. 'There's more than enough to charge him, then gather further proof afterwards. Hone up on your interviewing techniques. Are you charging him with the other murder?'

Blades did his best to keep his features as stony as he could, while he gave thought to his answer. 'It's more difficult to argue a case with that one. We can't place him there, and the murders may not have been done by the same person. Without witnesses that place him anywhere near the murder, a good defence lawyer would have that case dismissed.'

Moffat tutted and shifted papers on his desk. 'There were suggestions in the press that the first murder was committed by the same Ridges murderer as before. What do you think of that?'

'It's never been proved Pulteney didn't do the first two murders. The evidence we had against him at the time was strong enough to hang him.'

Moffat's questioning look was severe. 'And the third Ridges murder? He couldn't have done that. And, again, it was a young woman on the same stretch of beach. Elspeth

Summers, wasn't it? Another one killed by being hit over the head with a rock.'

'We like Robert for Daphne. Could he have done Elspeth as well? He was an occasional customer in the Victoria bar where she worked, though we can't establish a relationship with her.'

'Why the similarities with the murders of Anne Talbot and Jane Dawson, if the third was done by someone else?'

'A copycat? Either a random one or someone with a motive and relationship with Elspeth, who murdered her in such a way as to suggest it was our homicidal maniac again.'

'A bold thing to do with someone already convicted of the first two.'

Once again, Blades found himself faced with Moffat's glare. 'We could do more digging to establish whether Robert did more with Elspeth than just buy drinks from her.'

Blades did not like the look of doubt on Moffat's face as he gave thought to that before speaking again. 'You've a case against Robert for the murder of his sister.' And Blades noticed the assurance with which that was said.

'That's where we're heading, yes.'

'What you've said suggests a spur-of-the-moment crime, which may not tie in with a series of three murders.'

'Possibly not, but I think Robert probably did kill both Daphne and Jane Proudfoot,' Blades said, 'though we can't prove he murdered Jane at the moment. That doesn't mean we won't be able to. Possibly, he did murder Elspeth Summers but that was some time ago now. We may never get any further forward with that one.'

With a look of decisiveness, Moffat leaned forward and Blades realised that any doubts he had were to no avail now. It was just as well he did agree with him that Robert did it. 'All right. Charge Robert Tanner for the murder of his sister and look for evidence against him for the murder of Jane Proudfoot. Well done, Blades.'

Moffat now sat back again. The lines that had been so boldly drawn on his forehead had receded. A small smile appeared just at the edges of his mouth.

CHAPTER SEVENTEEN

After Robert was charged, Blades was left to turn his attention to the murder of Jane, which might turn up further links to Robert or might not. Constables were directed to renew door-to-door inquiries where Jane had lived and worked – and where she was murdered. Was there a witness they had missed? Had anyone seen something but not thought it important enough to mention?

There was a report from one witness, which said that Jane had been seen with someone whose description sounded a bit like Frank. That tied in with the account of someone seen near the Khyber Pass who also resembled Frank. Frank had said he hadn't anything to do with Jane for some time. If it could be proved he was lying about that, it would be interesting. Blades interviewed the witness but found that when he was asked to describe the person again, the description varied and did not sound much like Frank at all now.

Blades turned his attention to another report, one of a tramp who had been seen sleeping rough for a couple of nights near the Khyber Pass. The tramp had found a lock broken on a garden shed or had broken it himself. When the constable inspected the shed, he did find signs someone had been sleeping there. Tools had been cleared to make a space, and there was an empty meat tin, which suggested the presence of someone.

Blades ruminated on the connections this case seemed to be throwing up with tramps, then interviewed the witnesses. They had been shocked to discover a down-and-out living at the bottom of the garden. The lady of the house had gone out with washing for the line when she came across him. He had been sitting on the shed step quite the thing, enjoying the sunshine and a cigarette. She had dropped her washing basket and rushed back in for her husband, but by the time he was out the tramp was hot-footing it. He showed quite a bit of spryness in the way he hopped over the fence into their neighbour's garden, scrambled over the wall there, and disappeared into the alley leading to the High Street. They had not chased after him, being glad just to see the back of him. He had not returned. Blades asked for a description of the tramp, at which the couple simply looked at each other.

'I don't know,' the wife said.

'He was just like any tramp,' the husband said.

'There are a lot of those,' Blades replied, 'but can you think of anything that was distinctive about him?'

The husband frowned. 'Average sort of height.' He paused then said, 'Average sort of face. Weather-beaten, but then they all are.'

'Nothing unusual about the face? The nose? The ears?'

'He did have a nose,' the wife replied, 'but apart from that, I can't tell you anything about it. Sorry.'

The husband laughed. 'And he did have ears. But they didn't stick out or anything. They looked very ordinary ears to me, but then I saw him at a distance as he was running away.'

'I just dropped my basket when I saw him and went to fetch John.'

'Thin, fat, burly?' Blades asked.

'He was quite sturdy,' the wife replied.

'He was broad, but he didn't give the impression he had a lot of fat on him. Of course, he could have been like anything under that disgusting overcoat.'

'What was his hat like?' Blades asked.

'A slouch hat,' the husband replied. 'Brown, I suppose, like his coat.'

'He could run fast,' the wife said.

'He wasn't one you'd seen about before?' Blades asked.

'Wouldn't want to either,' they said, almost at the same time.

'How was he dressed?'

'An ancient-looking coat. Disgusting, it was.'

'Can you describe it?'

'Three-quarters length, and a bit ragged round the bottom.'

'Did he say anything?' Blades asked.

'Bugger off you lot,' the husband said.

'Charming, that was. It's our shed,' his wife added.

'Did you notice anything about the way he spoke?'

'Not that he said a lot,' the husband said, 'but it was clear enough. A northern sort of accent.'

'Thank you,' Blades said. Despite the couple's vagueness, one or two details had emerged. 'I'll get you to give a statement to the desk sergeant.'

After the husband and wife had left the interview room, he and Peacock looked at each other.

'That could be Len,' Peacock said. 'It's odd – here we are, trying to put Robert at two murders, and we might be able to place someone else altogether at them.'

'There is that tramp all the rest say they're terrified of.'

'He's a legend. He doesn't exist.'

'No one has suggested he might be Len?'

'Have we asked them?'

Blades thought of the shambling mess he had interviewed that had been Len and tried to picture him as the spry tramp who had legged it away so fast. It was probably some other one.

* * *

Len was always happy when he was on the road, and he was on it now, with Henry. Henry said he had never known any other life, not that Len knew whether to believe him or not, but he was learning a lot from Henry. Before they had left Birtleby, Henry had made a point of visiting a butcher, and Len noted that Henry did not beg but asked for two pennyworth of rough meat. Henry explained later to Len that butchers always have a piece of rough meat spare lying around that can't be sold, so it can be given to someone's dog, but Henry didn't see why a dog should get it when he could. And the butcher always had something else spare, so he added that to it. After that, Henry called at the greengrocer and asked if he could buy two potatoes. 'Is that all you want to buy from me?' the greengrocer asked, before looking Henry up and down, then giving him four, which he did not charge for.

After they had left Birtleby, they passed a field with carrots in it, and Henry helped himself to a couple there. Henry explained to Len that it would be good to have a pinch of tea as well, and a bit of sugar, so he called at a cottage he had visited previously. There was no one in, which was unfortunate, but he called at another one further on. He had not met the good lady there before, but she took pity on him and let him have some. She even let him have a few pence and an old shirt of her husband's. Further on, he called at yet another house to ask for some hot water for his billy can. There again, they decided they felt sorry for him and gave him what he asked for with a few pence on top. Henry had not let Len visit the cottages with him. If there were two of them it would be intimidating, he said, but he did explain later to Len what had transpired, and he shared what he had garnered. They were mates.

Why were they mates? Len supposed Henry had taken pity on him. Perhaps that was a luxury to a tramp. They found a quiet spot by a stream, and 'drummed up' there. Len made a fire with sticks he found lying around and brewed up with the water and tea that Henry had begged. Henry used his 'drum' to make stew. This was a half-pound coffee tin with two holes in the top for the string Henry used to carry it, and it was ideal for cooking the meat and potatoes he had assembled, and the carrots he had gleaned.

It was then that Henry told Len this was the only life he had ever known. 'You're fairly new to the road,' he said. 'You need an old hand to show you the ropes.'

From Len's point of view, it seemed he had been on the road for ever, but to an old stager like Henry it might not seem long.

'How do you cope with it?' Len asked.

'I love it,' Henry replied.

From him, Len was beginning to discover there could be more things to savour still than he had thought.

Henry explained to him that the next spike was one to be avoided. The porter was mean and made you labour like a slave in return for the shelter you got. And what kind of shelter was it? And what kind of food? It was easier to beg a good stew like they had that day, wasn't it? And more comfortable sleeping in a haystack than on a hard floor. That night, Henry found them a good going hayrick, and Len agreed with him.

It was during the night that it happened. Len had been dreaming. He was back at the Front, and the guns were firing their shells, and machine guns were sending tracers overhead, and the fear and anger was thrumming right through him again. He was aware of the tread of a foot beside him and turned to parry the thrust of a bayonet from a German who must have crawled over on night patrol. Len launched himself in his direction, there was a scream, and Len woke up to find himself on top of Henry, and thwacking his fist into him, with poor Henry begging for mercy. Len pulled his arm back, stood up, and stepped away. Henry stared at Len from his position on the ground.

'You, mad fool,' he said. 'You're not all there. After what I've tried to do for you. Stay away from me.'

Then Henry was gathering his things together and trudging off, leaving Len on his own. Len felt ever so guilty about the way he had behaved towards Henry, but he told himself he couldn't be the only person who was like that after the war, could he? He had heard of shellshock, whatever it was, and sometimes wondered if that was what he had. It left him alone for long enough. Why did it have to come back? Maybe it would just go away sometime and never return. He could only hope for that. Every so often, he thought back to Henry and his mind lingered with regret over the contentment that he and Henry seemed to have found on the road.

CHAPTER EIGHTEEN

Blades was seated in the Proudfoots' best room –
dominated by its piano and photographs of different
generations of Proudfoots looking sternly ahead. After
questioning Jane's mother, he had come to the conclusion
that, helpful as she might be, she was too much of a
matriarch to know as much about her daughter's life as she
thought she did. Blades asked her if he could speak to
Jane's sister Ethel on her own. Mrs Proudfoot's face
showed grave reservations, but she agreed, and Ethel now
sat opposite Blades and Peacock, a prim expression on her
face. She held herself upright as she looked them in the
eye.

'We haven't been able to find out much about Jane,'
Blades said. 'We know she worked in a shop. She was
young and attractive. She had girlfriends she mixed with at
her sewing circle. Everyone liked her and speaks well of
her. She was a paragon totally without enemies, who
happened to find herself in the wrong place at the wrong
time. There must be more to your sister than that.'

Ethel's mouth showed a trace of a sardonic smile now,
and her eyebrows raised slightly.

'Can you help us find her killer?' Blades asked.

'What do you want to know?' Ethel asked.

'Can you tell us anything about any men she might have known?' Peacock asked.

Ethel's face was thoughtful as she looked curiously back at Peacock, then across to Blades.

'Someone must have shown an interest in her,' Blades said.

Ethel's eyes flashed briefly as she seemed to reach a decision. 'There was one young man. His name was George Bright. He was a good-looking man and I wasn't half jealous of her – but he died. When was it the war ended? At the eleventh hour on the eleventh day of the eleventh month 1918. Such an arithmetically pretty time to decide on. A sniper's bullet took him at five to eleven.'

Ethel's expression was fixed as she said this, though Blades had the impression of powerful feelings underneath.

Ethel continued. 'We told her not to waste her own life. She couldn't mourn him forever. He wouldn't have wanted that. He thought so much of her. He loved her. But we couldn't get her to look at anyone else, not that there's a huge choice after the war. They're all either dead or damaged. What's a girl to make of that?'

Blades was working out what was hidden behind Ethel's front, grief for her sister, yes – but also bitterness. He could see it in the set of those lips and that sharp look in the eye.

'But do you know who she fell for?' Ethel said. 'That Frank Bywaters, that's who. I wouldn't have given him the time of day, someone too cowardly to go out there and do his duty, but she went for him.'

'Was she seeing him?'

'He was that taken up with Daphne he wouldn't look at her. There was no reason why he shouldn't be happy with Daphne. She was all right, and if she'd look at the likes of him, he was lucky. But that left Jane out of things. I told her to forget about Frank. He was taken. Jane did have the common sense to accept it, and she never went near him. But we're sisters. I knew she still couldn't get him out of her mind.'

'Did she see him after Daphne was killed?' Blades asked.

'Now, there's a thing. I suppose that was an opportunity for her. I told her not to bother. He was no man. If he could let his country down, he could let her down. But can you credit it? She liked the fact he was a CO. She wanted a man of peace after the horrors of the war. I told her it would just be a rebound for him, and her, but she didn't care. So, yes. She would have taken up with him if she'd had the chance. But she didn't see him, as far as I know. Is that any help?'

'Had her behaviour changed in any way?' Blades asked.

'I didn't always know what she was up to. She didn't always tell me.'

'Do you think she could have arranged to see him after going to her sewing circle?'

'They didn't finish at any set time and she didn't have to be in by any particular hour, so she could have been having secret assignations as far as anyone knew. But if she was coming back from seeing Frank, it still doesn't help you. It doesn't tell you who murdered her.'

'It couldn't have been Frank who killed her?' Peacock asked.

'He was a CO,' Ethel said. 'He wouldn't kill anyone. That was his problem.' Then, her face transformed into one of anger as the pitch of her voice changed. 'If he did, he's a bloody hypocrite. You make sure you get him. I want him hanged if he did that.'

'We can't convict him on conjecture,' Blades said, 'which is all this is. You didn't come across any notes or hear her say anything that suggested she was seeing Frank?'

'She was still burning a torch for him. If he'd asked her to go out with him, she would have said yes.' The sudden flare of anger had gone, but a lot of indignation remained in that voice.

'Do you know if she ever did arrange to see him?'

Ethel thought. 'No. But she did go a bit dreamy at times, so she might have had someone. She was so low after George was killed, and I mean for a long time after, but lately she'd been much more cheerful. It was good to see.'

Then she stopped talking as she thought of this some more.

'Someone was cheering her up?' Peacock asked.

'If it was Frank, she might not have told me.' Ethel's tone was thoughtful.

'Would she have told you if she'd been seeing Robert?' Blades asked.

'Robert? You don't think she would have looked at him, do you? I hear you arrested him for the murder of his sister. Do you think he could have killed Jane as well?'

'Someone did,' Blades replied. 'But we have no witnesses placing him near Jane's murder, and he has an alibi.'

'And I don't know anything about him seeing Jane.'

After they left Ethel, Blades muttered to himself. Information was always the same, suggestive but not conclusive. 'I wish Jane wasn't such an elusive person,' he said to Peacock. 'She was unusually cheerful. Why? Her sister says she supposes Jane could have been seeing someone. Or not. If she was, Ethel doesn't know who it might have been.'

'Did anyone in Jane's family know her?' Peacock asked.

'You might wonder,' Blades replied.

* * *

Blades and Peacock questioned the young women in Jane's sewing circle further. The one they were talking to now was a bold-eyed girl with a well-sculpted, blonde Marcel Wave and a confident way of holding herself.

'Jane was definitely seeing Frank,' Ruth told them. 'She saw him once, anyway. I told her she was a scarlet woman approaching him like that, but she said she couldn't help herself. And there she was, out at the sea-front walking with him, quite the thing when I saw her. Anyone could have seen her. I'm surprised no one else has told you this. Saturday, it was.'

'We have talked to other people she knew, including all the other women in that sewing circle,' Blades said. 'And no one else has mentioned this.'

'She told me about him. Told me to keep it under my hat. So I did. Then I saw her out and about with him, bold as brass. I wondered why I'd bothered.'

Blades almost laughed. Just like that. A link between Frank and Jane. So much for witnesses coming forward in answer to appeals in newspapers. So much for constables going about in the vicinity, asking questions. Jane had strolled right along the seafront with Frank and nobody noticed.

'It was her family she didn't want to find out. There would be trouble. A conchie? After Jane losing her fiancé in that war – and her brother dying in it? But that's why Jane said she wanted one. She didn't want anyone who'd been mixed up in all that killing. I told her that was warped, and that she should put all that behind her and get a decent bloke. But he had a way with him, I suppose, and Jane fell for it.'

Blades tried to stop himself gaping at her as she said all this.

'But you don't think Frank killed Jane, do you?' she said.

'I don't know,' Blades replied. 'We're trying to piece together different threads of evidence, that's all. We did think Jane might have been seeing someone. You're the one who says it was Frank. Does it mean he killed her? You tell us. Do you think that's likely, going by what you know?'

Ruth's face looked perplexed. Then it looked piqued. 'So, why do you think Frank did it?' she asked. 'Who'd have thought that of Frank? Well, I never. And he always looked such an innocent, as if he was not quite in this world. Why do you think he did it?'

Blades did not reply. He asked her to give her statement to a constable and left her with him. Ruth might be jumping to conclusions, but he should not.

When he returned to his office, he found more reports from constables, even one which also pointed the finger at Frank. Someone else had seen Frank with Jane on the sea-front on Saturday. Blades thought that witness report had taken long enough to come in, but at least it was there. Then Blades' eyes were drawn to another one. A man answering Frank's description had been seen walking away from the Khyber Pass on the night of Jane's murder. Someone else had seen Frank near there that night. Were they building a case against Frank? They would question him and see. If they had a case against Robert for the murder of Daphne, and succeeded in compiling one against Frank for the murder of Jane, did that cover everything? Or was there something they had missed? Birtleby. There seemed to be something hanging over it. Why did so many deaths happen here? It was not a big town. And they were all young women. Was there some curse on the place, or some spirit lurking about seeking vengeance? But Blades rejected these as fanciful thoughts.

CHAPTER NINETEEN

'Robert Tanner has a lawyer.'

The words themselves were not a surprise to Blades. What was alarming was that Chief Constable Moffat had summoned him so that Blades could listen to them.

'He is entitled to one, sir' was the obvious reply, but Blades did wish that he had not said it.

'He has told me that under no circumstances should this case have been presented against his client.'

'We discussed the evidence, sir, and you said you were satisfied with it.'

'It sounded reasonable as you presented it.'

'As I presented it?'

'Two of your witnesses are vagabonds.'

'Does that mean they should be ignored, sir? Just because they're derelicts does not mean that they are telling lies.'

'A jury will not believe them without corroboration.'

'But we have it. The word of a respectable member of the community – a tailor.'

'A man with a known grudge against Robert Tanner. Just what do you think a defence lawyer will make of that in a courtroom? That witness was in a fight with Robert only a week before.'

'I didn't know about any fight.'

'But it is your job to already be aware of that. That lawyer is. Why didn't you talk to Robert's family about him as well? And a lot of other people saw the fight and heard what was said. Why didn't you turn them up? One-armed or not, Robert beat the living daylights out of him. That would make anyone resent Robert.'

Blades thought about reminding Moffat he had questioned whether they had conclusive proof against Robert at the time, but Moffat could be unpredictable, and he doubted if it would be wise.

'Of course, sir.'

'Robert Tanner is to be released immediately,' Moffat said.

Stronger words occurred to Blades, but he bit them back. 'Yes, sir,' he said.

'I take it you found no further evidence against him, nothing conclusive, or anything of that ilk?'

'Nothing further, sir, no.'

'And nothing links him to the Jane Proudfoot inquiry?'

'No, sir.'

Moffat shuffled some papers. At least his fury seemed to be spent for the moment. Now a look almost of helplessness had come over him. 'There's nothing resembling a case against anyone else, I suppose?'

Blades thought of their leads in the Jane Proudfoot investigation, but they were not established well enough to mention to someone as impatient as Moffat.

Moffat continued. 'Two young women have been murdered in Birtleby. Someone is stalking the streets of the town, which means women are too terrified to even step out of the door. We need to do something about that. Wouldn't you agree?'

'Of course, sir. We are pursuing inquiries. We do follow up leads.'

'What leads do you have?'

'They haven't led to anything substantial yet,' Blades said.

'Obviously not.' The look Moffat gave Blades was withering. 'It's time that homicidal maniac was caught.'

'Yes, sir.'

Arguments against Moffat arose in Blades' mind, but what he needed was the murderer and he did not have him. He had to admit to being surprised by that account of Robert beating someone to pulp with only one arm – and two powerful legs, Blades could only suppose. When he thought of it, Robert did look as if he had a good kick on him. Blades wondered why Moffat did not consider this made Robert an even more plausible suspect instead of exonerating him. Moffat was now assuming a homicidal maniac was at large, something that everyone in Birtleby probably thought as well, but which, to Blades, was one theory only. What proof was there of it? If only he had bucket-loads of that, Blades thought. If only someone could manage to spot the murderer in the act and come forward with a statement about that. Then a thought occurred to Blades. Suppose he could arrange things so that someone did?

* * *

When Peacock heard Blades' suggestion, he blinked twice then laughed. Embarrassed by his own reaction, Peacock apologised. 'I did not mean… You took me by surprise. But when I think about it–' He paused and gave it more thought. 'Would Moffat go for that?' he said.

'Leave him to me,' Blades said.

'You know his opinion of women in the police force. Good for making tea and comforting children. And not much else.'

'There are two women police constables in Leeds now,' Blades said. 'One of them could be seconded for this.'

'It would be asking her to take a dreadful risk.'

'We would have policemen nearby. We would look after her. At the first sound of her whistle, half a dozen able-bodied policemen would be on the man.'

'I suppose,' Peacock said. 'On the other hand, our murderer might never turn up. We could have her staked out for six months patrolling the Ridges on the off-chance he would appear, and he might never oblige.'

'It's following up the theory of the homicidal maniac. We haven't properly explored that one. We assume, for once, Pulteney did not do the first two murders but that all five were committed by the same man. We then look at the times and places of all five murders and look for common factors. That tells us where and when to place her – and it might give us a very good chance of catching him.'

'You know what Moffat's like on finances. This will cost money.'

'He's in a panic after what Robert Tanner's lawyer said to him. He'll agree to this alright, particularly if the *Birtleby Times* gets up in arms about things. And we can get them primed.'

'You could?'

'And the *Leeds Chronicle*. This is more their style.'

'Don't do that. It could backfire. You're the investigating officer. You could end up being called a lot of things.'

'We need to catch this murderer.'

'We do.' Then Peacock became thoughtful. 'I doubt if one homicidal maniac did all five.'

'Our other theories haven't led us anywhere.'

'I still think you were right about Pulteney doing the first two murders. But one person could have done the other three, and my money's on Robert.'

'There are three theories,' Blades said. 'Theory A – a homicidal maniac did the lot, which this ploy will test. B – Robert did at least one, if not two or three. C – Frank did one, if not two or three. And by laying this trap we might even catch either of them.'

'And if it doesn't work?'

'It doesn't. But if it does, it will provide cast-iron proof, and that would be worth having.'

'It would,' Peacock said, and he gave Blades what was supposed to be a smile, but Blades could only see the doubt in his eyes.

* * *

ONLY SUSPECT RELEASED

Birtleby Police Force has failed once again to make any progress in their investigations into the recent murders of Daphne Tanner and Jane Proudfoot. They have now had to release their only suspect, Robert Tanner, the brother of Daphne. One can but feel for a brother mourning his sister who finds himself accused of her murder. This newspaper is surprised at the slightness of the case the police were considering, one based on the witness statements of two indigents, and a man with a known grudge against Robert Tanner. This was a man who had been in a physical altercation with him only a week before. One can only consider how desperate Birtleby Police must have been to take such a case against Robert Tanner seriously. This is a man who fought in the trenches for this country, a man who has two campaign medals for his part in our victory. Is this how we should be treating our heroes? He not only risked his life but gave an arm. Robert Tanner was a tailor before he went out to the trenches but cannot now pursue that trade because of his injuries. So many of our young men came back damaged from that war. Who has not seen crippled veterans on street corners trying to sell pencils or pens or thread or anything appropriate in order to feed and clothe themselves? Why do we neglect them? And why do we add to the woes of such as Robert Tanner?

Major questions ought to be asked about the conduct of this investigation. A murderer has stalked Birtleby for the last two years, killing five young women. There has been nothing like this since the days of Jack the Ripper. Birtleby Police Force has hanged one innocent man already, William Pulteney. We know that because the murders have simply continued after that execution. And they were about to try another. When are they going to convict the actual killer?

'At least, you weren't named that time,' Peacock said.

'Thank God for that,' Blades said, 'but it was a risk worth taking. Moffat has agreed to have a female constable seconded from Leeds. With a decent slice of luck, we'll catch the man.'

CHAPTER TWENTY

Like other women in the police, Florence Smithson had started off the war in a voluntary unit, but she was a full-time member of Leeds Police now. Women police patrols had been a novelty when they were initiated, and Florence had met distrust from the public, even mockery; she had also to negotiate the disbelieving and patronising reactions of the policemen she worked beside; and her family disapproved. But Florence was determined to succeed in this job. She had started off working in London and had formed one half of a two-woman patrol in which she found herself having to adapt quickly.

Florence had spent her entire life until then, well-sheltered from unpleasantness and had been educated in a private school for young ladies, before being sent to a finishing school in Paris. But she had wanted to do her bit in the war, and this was something that women could do. Hers was a patriotic family. Her brother had been one of the first to volunteer in 1914 and had served as an officer. He was also one of the first to die in battle, but his memory was kept alive in Florence's household, and Florence decided that she wanted to live up to it.

There was a variety of tasks that women volunteered for but knitting socks for the men at the Front held no appeal for Florence, nor did organizing food parcels. Florence had been a suffragette before war broke out and breaking new frontiers for women appealed to her. Like some others from the former suffragette army, Florence helped found the Women Patrols.

Patrolling London parks involved meeting situations previously well beyond her ken. A lot of the work consisted of separating cavorting couples. Once Florence had even come across a man straddling another man. That was difficult for her, but she did find it satisfying to help young women who found themselves in difficult circumstances. In all of this, Florence's education and class stood her in good stead. The people she came across on patrol were usually of the common class, who respected the authority of her vowels at least. Now, she found herself in Blades' parlour being studied by him.

He was impressed. She may only have been five foot six, but she was strongly built, and looked a force to be reckoned with. Her hair was cut short and, as she was wearing her police uniform, a neat blue costume with leggings, she gave a manly impression. The naturally stern expression on her face was the result of her numerous Women's Police patrols, Blades assumed, but she did return his welcoming smile with warmth. He noticed her delicate feminine airs had not entirely deserted her as she sat holding one of Jean's finest bone china teacups and simpered in her direction.

'Beautiful china,' Florence said. 'I'm glad I've arrived in civilisation.'

'You're more than welcome here,' Jean said.

'We'll see if the men are welcoming in that police station,' Florence replied.

'I should hope they are,' Jean said, sending Blades a stern look.

'They're not always,' Florence said. 'I've been told to get back to my washtub before now.' But Florence laughed at this. 'Policemen. The looks on some of their faces when they see me.' She laughed again.

Blades said, 'I'll tell the men to be on their best behaviour. And before you say anything, Jean, I was the one who asked for Florence's help. I know what she's worth.'

'I should hope so,' Jean said.

'It's good to be wanted,' Florence said. 'A lot of the men thought at the end of the war, oh good – we can get rid of women police now.'

'Did they?' Jean said. 'I wonder why you bothered staying on.'

'I wasn't going anywhere. We showed them we can do a good job.'

'I entirely agree,' Blades said, thinking he would have to be particularly careful in how he treated Florence as it would all get back to Jean.

'What is it she's being asked to do here?' Jean asked.

'Oh that,' Blades said. He sipped tea while he struggled to find the right words to explain this.

'You'd be surprised what they ask us to do,' Florence said. 'Quite right too, though. There should have been women in the police years ago. At least I can arrest people now.'

'You're with the police. Isn't that taken for granted?' Jean asked.

'When we first started, we had to get a helpful policeman to do the arresting for us. It's still the case in London.'

'What did they use you for there?'

'We did a lot of work with prostitutes. The older women don't want to know anything about us, but we can help the younger ones, though they might not see it as that. We charge them with insulting behaviour. That gets them away from the madams, and there's no stigma attached to the charge. They haven't been arrested for prostitution as such. Some of them manage to get back to a normal life after that.'

'Which has to be a good thing,' Blades said. 'It's difficult to get them to listen to men. They don't trust them.'

'I don't blame them,' Florence said. 'You should see what I've seen.'

Blades gave her a questioning look.

'And we take statements from women who have been victims of sexual crimes,' Florence continued.

'That's a good idea,' Jean said. 'Imagine having to talk about that to a man.'

'But things can be different when they get to court. If some judges have their way, they won't allow any other women in the courtroom when a woman is giving evidence. Imagine that. Testifying about some dreadful outrage in front of an entirely male jury, a male judge, prosecuting counsel and all the rest of them – because listening to that sort of thing's not supposed to be fit for the delicacies of the female. We have made progress. A woman member of the police is present at a lot of cases now. But some judges are notorious. They still won't allow it.'

Jean looked impressed by what Florence was saying. 'You take pride in what you're doing,' she said, 'and it all sounds like difficult work.'

'Absolutely,' Florence said.

'What is it Stephen wants you to help with here?'

Florence echoed Blades' earlier response. 'Oh that,' she said. She and Blades looked at each other. 'When there are attacks on women in an area, they sometimes use us as decoys to trap the man. Like here.'

A horrified look came over Jean's face.

'You're not using her for that?' Jean said. 'Look at her. She's not the sort of young lady who should be used for that.'

'Oh, I'm happy about it,' Florence said. 'I volunteered when I heard they wanted a woman police officer to help trap your Ridges murderer. That man needs to be caught.'

'Really?' Jean said, but her face still looked doubtful.

'Women police are trained to defend themselves,' Blades said. 'Florence is particularly adept at ju-jitsu, aren't you? I wouldn't advise anyone to attack her.'

'I could get a man down and hold him in complete agony till the troops arrived,' Florence said.

Blades himself blanched when she said that.

'And there will be plenty of big burly policemen close at hand,' he said to Jean. 'There will be no danger to Florence.' Which he hoped with all of his heart was true.

* * *

'I have served as bait before.'

Blades was in his office, with Florence and Peacock. Florence was trying to persuade Peacock that this was something she could take in her stride.

'You have?' Peacock was giving her a surprised look. 'Bait for what?'

'There was a series of rapes in Hyde Park. A volunteer was asked for and I stepped forward.'

'Why?' Peacock asked.

'I wanted the man to be caught.'

'I suppose that makes sense, but weren't you afraid?'

'Who wouldn't be?' Florence said. 'But I knew the risk. I'm trained in self-defence and the use of my police whistle, and I had enough male colleagues standing by.'

'What happened?' Peacock asked.

'We caught him.'

Blades liked Florence's blunt replies; they suggested a direct and honest approach to her policework – and nerve.

'I didn't come to any harm. When he came up behind me, I flipped him over and held him. You never saw such a surprised look as the one on his face. I enjoyed that.

Then two constables rushed forward and put him in cuffs. Are the constables here any good?'

'Very, and they'd better be, with you putting yourself on the line like this,' Blades replied. 'And Peacock and I will be there as well.'

As there were no women in Birtleby Police, Peacock had no experience of them. Blades knew he would have heard about them from officers in other areas, who were prone to say that women were too slightly built for police work and that they only added to a policeman's duties because he had to protect his colleague; and it was a view Blades knew that Peacock shared. Now Peacock found himself looking at Florence, and Blades could see he was wondering whether to revise his opinions.

'Do you know where and when you're putting me?' Florence asked Blades.

'It's worked out,' Blades replied.

'Where do the attacks take place?'

'Mostly on the Ridges.'

'Is there a common time?'

'Mid-afternoon to early evening mostly, though the last one was later than that, and in a different place. He attacks his women when they are by themselves in a lonely spot. We think he follows them there. Sometimes they've started off in the company of a young man before they parted company. Sometimes they seem to have gone there by themselves.'

'What are the women like?'

'Younger than you, in point of fact. Late teens, early twenties. But it shouldn't matter. You can dress yourself to look younger and put on make-up. You're attractive, and, as long as you're by yourself, he'll attack alright.'

'Nothing to worry about, then.'

'If you like to look at it that way,' Blades said. He and Florence exchanged weak grins.

'How many has he killed?'

Blades pondered. 'It's difficult to say. There have been five victims, but that doesn't mean they were all done by the same person. To the best of our knowledge, only three were. Someone was convicted for the first two: the wrong man, if you are to believe the press – but I don't think so.'

'But he's had practice?'

'Yes.'

'How does he kill them?'

'Any blunt object to hand, usually a rock, though one victim was killed with a knife.'

'That could have been somebody else?'

'And it was done away from the Ridges, so the answer to that is that we don't know. We just follow through on theories. In point of fact, there's too much we don't know, and the press are making the most of that and terrifying every young woman for miles around. We need to catch this man. You can be a real help to us.'

'I hope it works. When do we start?'

'Tomorrow. We'll have you walking along the sea-front with a young man tomorrow afternoon, holding hands and laughing. That seems to start something off in our murderer. Then you can have a quarrel and your young man can leave you there, which is when you start walking off by yourself into the Ridges. The men will be staked out. He won't see them, but they'll see him – and you. We'll make sure you're safe.'

'Sounds all right. Who's the young man I go canoodling with?'

'Someone's being sent over from Linfrith. You'll meet him tomorrow.'

'I hope he's handsome.'

Blades laughed. 'I've never met him myself. I'm told he's a good man for the job, but how good-looking I don't know. He is the same age as you.'

Now that she knew the plans, Florence looked more relaxed. She grinned. 'I've never been on a blind date before. This'll be interesting. But he'd better keep his hands to himself or I'll be practising my ju-jitsu on him.'

'Sounds fair enough. But don't worry. He will behave. Oh and–'

'What?'

'Wear a short dress. Our killer seems to like those. And make-up.'

'I'll get to wear make-up on duty? That'll make a change. Do you have any idea who the killer is?'

'Possibly. Or at least any one of three – we think.'

'What makes you think he'll be about tomorrow?'

'He might not be. We might need to stage this a few times.'

'I hope my blind date doesn't get bored with me.'

Blades laughed. 'I doubt it.'

* * *

Blades and Peacock were seated, binoculars beside them, in a deserted part of the dunes in the middle of a patch of marram grass. Officers had stood in different places to check the two could not be spotted. There were now policemen hidden in the dunes on either side of the track leading from the sea-front, with others stationed further on. It was approaching three and Blades was satisfied they had done as much as they could to be ready.

It was a dull day with low clouds that held a suggestion of rain in them. Blades hoped it would stay clear. He was wondering whether Florence and her companion, Jack, were in position yet. He supposed they were, and that they were already strolling hand in hand.

Blades pondered who the killer would turn out to be. With Robert's bitterness and short temper, Blades still thought he was the likely bet. Possibly, Moffat had protected the innocent when he had dropped the charge against Robert – or not. Robert could be now pretending to stroll casually behind Florence and Jack. Robert was a self-obsessed young man who did not show much awareness of the emotions of others, the type who might very well commit murder without a thought. Life had treated him badly, and Blades supposed Robert might feel he had the right to exact revenge on someone else. And a young woman could fit the bill, one of the gender who had handed out white feathers to force young men out into the hell of the trenches while they stayed safe at home. Robert's life had ended when that bullet had hit his arm. It might have been kinder to him if he had died. Then he would not have had to endure the excruciating pity of others, and the lack of hope. He was alive, but his future was dead. That was something someone like Robert could take out on a woman, any woman. And if he had done it once, it would be so easy to do it again. When that bitterness rose up in him again, he would make another kill. If Robert turned up and attacked Florence with his one arm and two strong legs, it would not surprise Blades.

Or Frank might arrive in a frenzy and attack her. Blades did think that possible from this conscientious objector. There was a self-obsession about him, and a preference for ideas over people. To what extent did Frank understand the way other people's minds worked? To what extent did that matter to him? Perhaps it would not be difficult for someone like him to kill someone. It might be like erasing an idea he had written on a page. Blades did not know what made people like Frank snap, but he could imagine it would be difficult for Daphne or anybody else if they happened to be there. And Jane? Why would he have snapped at Jane? Perhaps she had tried to wrench him away from his ideas and into physicality. Blades hoped this musing would soon be over and their killer exposed in the act. Blades did not think he had any real understanding of someone like Frank and what might make him kill or not. Only Frank understood Frank, so yes, it might be him for reasons that were too clever for ordinary people like Blades to follow.

Then again, perhaps when they hanged Pulteney they had hanged an innocent man. Perhaps all five murders had been done by one person, their local homicidal maniac, the tramp who passed en route through his area. Tramps did come and go all the time, with no one keeping real track of them. And they were broken men, with anything they had possessed in the world taken from them. Why not strip everything away from someone else? It could even be Len, or Jed, for all Blades knew, though he suspected that if this was the work of the sinister tramp the others spoke of, he had not met him yet.

One thing for sure was that someone malevolent existed out here. Created out of what? The damage the Great War had wreaked on some soldiers' psyche? Or even the damage the Great War had done to the psyche of Birtleby? Perhaps the 'war to end all wars' still lurked out here, seeking vengeance for itself by breaking out again in different ex-soldiers' skulls. Blades mourned what had been created by that conflict. His eyes searched round, seeking the demon that man had made, but all that he could see was sand, and air, and waves. Then he dismissed his feverish fancies, raised his binoculars and scanned the Ridges for Florence.

He spotted her almost straight away. She was still far off, not close to them yet, but he could just catch the sound of her laughter as she walked hand in hand with Jack. Slowly, they walked so slowly, but along they came. He heard their voices, as chatter weaved in and out between them. The breeze touched Blades' skin and his hand fingered the sand underneath him. A gull cawed and Blades continued to hold the glasses against his eyes as he stared at the couple. Then the voices changed. Their cheerful rhythm had disrupted itself, become ragged, even savage as they began to disagree, then shout at each other. Then, they parted, striding off in high dudgeon in their different planned directions. Florence strutted off into the beckoning Ridges as Blades and Peacock and the other policemen pointed their glasses and stared after her. Blades noticed the unconscious feminine sway of her body was in action, that signal to their unhinged killer, whoever it was, out there.

* * *

'Can you tell that nice constable to keep his hands to himself in future?' Florence moaned to Blades.

She was seated now at Jean's kitchen table with Blades and Jean. There was a flat mood in the room, as Blades and Florence were both deflated by the day's lack of success in tempting their killer.

'Constable Johnstone?'

'That's it. Jack. There's enthusiasm for the role and then there's taking advantage of it. Perhaps we should be doing a stake-out to catch Jack?'

'You mean he misbehaved?' Jean said. 'Stephen, that's terrible. You're not going to allow that?'

'I'll speak to him,' Blades said.

'And there was no sign of the other maniac after all that,' Florence said.

'It's an off-chance operation,' Blades said. 'We had no reason to believe he would strike today. And, having organized this, we will be continuing.'

'How long for?' Florence asked.

'A number of factors will decide that, expense for one thing, and other commitments. Then there's politics. Chief Constable Moffat will have something to say about it.'

'Do we know what the suspects did with themselves today?'

'Oh yes. We're watching them. They led perfectly innocent days. Suspect one was out and about looking for work. Suspect two was at work in the morning and busy with preparation and marking in the afternoon, we assume. He didn't leave the house anyway.'

'Suspect three?'

'A bit more anomalous. We know the type we suspect but not the man.'

'So, you won't cancel a day's operation just because suspect one and two are both innocently occupied?'

'No. You're all right with continuing with this?'

'He's a monster. I definitely want to catch this one.'

'Good. Glad to hear it.'

Blades liked what he heard from Florence. A policewoman who brooked no nonsense from her colleagues was someone with the sort of spirit that could be relied upon.

'You must be tired out,' Jean said to Florence. 'Are you sure you aren't asking her to do too much?' she asked her husband.

Florence grinned at her. 'Nothing will stop me doing this.'

'If anything happens to Florence, I'll hold you to blame,' Jean told Blades.

'We'll make sure she's safe.'

'I hope you're using big strapping constables, not spindly teenage trainees.'

'Sturdy coppers for a stout-hearted copperette,' Blades said.

'God. I haven't heard that term since I was in London,' Florence said.

'Some wag put the words suffragette and copper together, I think,' Blades explained to his wife.

'It was an insult,' Florence said, 'but I always liked it.'

'You were a suffragette?' Jean said.

'Absolutely. A bit of a change from fighting the boys in blue to becoming one, but the war changed everything.'

'You had fist fights with the police?' Blades said. 'I didn't know that.'

'Only the one arrest,' Florence said.

'Just the one?' Blades said. 'Usually that debars you from police work of any kind.'

'War broke out,' Florence said. 'A different one. There was an amnesty. Saved Westminster windows from me. Lucky them.'

Blades frosty look at Florence did not meet Jean's approval.

'She's putting her life on the line for you.' Jean said. 'Isn't that enough?'

Blades thought of a retort but dismissed it. 'She's brave enough,' he said. 'That's what we need. Thank you, Florence.'

But doubts had been placed in Blades' mind. He wasn't sure about Florence's cheerfulness at breaking the law, even if she did really believe in her cause. Perhaps it was just as well she had been seconded to Birtleby just for one operation.

'I think you're a very brave woman,' Jean said to Florence before giving a threatening look to Blades. 'If you have any trouble with him, let me know.'

Then Florence laughed. She looked different after today's duties. Despite the obvious stress of them, she was now again at ease, as if the familiarity with the task she had to do had reassured her. Blades appreciated the naturalness and the light in the eyes. There was a refreshing honesty about Florence. Perhaps she would be all right.

'You've the morning off tomorrow,' Blades told her. 'Make the most of it. You report to the station at one.'

Then he sat back in his seat and tried to relax.

CHAPTER TWENTY-ONE

The morning's headlines still blazed in Blades' mind. '*Letter From The Ridges Murderer. Birtleby Police Clueless Again.*' Who could have predicted that? Someone had written into the *Leeds Chronicle* claiming to have committed all five murders. Automatic credence could not be placed on this, and Blades noticed that the article contained no details that had not already been released to the public, but the *Leeds Chronicle* had published its article, without first putting it past him, or giving him the chance of investigating the letter. When he had the chance, he would follow up on that. What was even more annoying was that Blades found himself wondering, despite the obvious reservations, if the letter could have been from their man. Even when Blades was back at his watcher's post in the dunes beside Peacock as per schedule, his mind would not stop dwelling on that.

Blades and Peacock peered through their binoculars. This waiting was difficult. Would anything happen? Or would Blades find himself with more egg on his face? What would be the reaction of Moffat if he did? It was a bright day, sunlight glancing off the scudding waves. There was warmth on their skins. It was a pity about the chore they were on. This would be a good place to lie back and forget about things.

Blades thought of the men he had detailed to keep an eye on Robert and Frank. He wondered if Robert was already on his way to the Ridges. If he wasn't guilty, they had harassed an innocent man at a difficult time for him, and Blades would feel bad about that. What was Frank doing now? He had been mocked all through the war and after it for being a conchie, but at least he had the guts to stand up for his principles. Was he another shattered man whom they'd been bullying? Blades' mind went to Pulteney. At least he had been guilty, hadn't he? They had hanged him.

Blades had been convinced at the time that Pulteney had committed the first two murders, and he hoped so, though someone else was out there now, stalking Birtleby's young women. Which suspect was it? And had one man even done all three of these killings?

Blades thought of the offer that Jean's father had made after the murder of Elspeth Summers, amid the controversy about supposedly hanging the wrong man. That offer had never been withdrawn. Blades could walk away from all of this into a much less stressful job, manage a store, and life would become routine and safe. On the other hand, was safe what he wanted? Blades knew that, despite everything, there was something here he enjoyed. The rush of adrenaline was thrilling, and it was the uncertainty that brought it about. He wanted to arrest the maniac murderer and make Birtleby safe for young women again. That would be worth doing.

He thought of Florence and envied her. There was a young woman with real commitment, and not only was she carving out a career for herself, and burning out a path for other young women, she was out to make the world better for them. She had a cause, just as the men who had fought on the Front had one, one that had passed Blades by when he committed to the police instead, and which he had never stopped feeling guilty about. But he was on a cause now, just as much as Florence. He liked women, in particular Jean, and, though he had never met any of these young women who had been murdered, he instinctively knew he would have liked them. They were going about their lives, being cheerful and optimistic, looking for lightness and fun, enjoying the innocence of the moment. What right did anyone have to take that away from them?

He peered through his binoculars, and it was then that he saw them, Florence and Constable Johnstone, who had been told to behave today. They were hand in hand, full of the apparent joy of each other, though Blades knew that, on Florence's part, that was feigned.

CHAPTER TWENTY-TWO

Everything was annoying Robert today. His porridge had been tasteless, his coffee bitter, and even the brightness of the morning angered him. There was a cheerfulness about it that found no echo in him. This was on account of a person called Albert Tomkins, whom Robert had had an interview with the day before about a job in the post office in Linfrith, and despite the fact Robert had been offered it. It was all very well for his father to extol Albert's virtues. He had only met him in his expansive moods on post workers' social occasions when he was relaxing, which was how Pete had managed to inveigle an interview for a job as postman and sorter for his son.

Robert hadn't even been sure he wanted the work. It was not a bad job, but could he manage it? How easy would it be to sort letters with one arm? Or even balance a mail bag and pull out letters to deliver them? He knew anyone with two arms would do it much more quickly. Robert's father had told Robert to make sure he told Albert about his war-time experience, and the medals he had returned with. If Robert could do his duty when the shells were dropping, he could deliver letters in every weather. Robert thought it sounded more like playing on someone else's patriotism, and charity, though when he heard the pay offered, he thought he should worry about that less. This was not an altruistic job offer.

When Robert met Albert face to face as a prospective employee in his post office, he noticed Albert's eye never once left Robert's empty sleeve. It was easy enough to envisage what that calculating look encompassed. How much longer would it take Robert to complete a job? How much less could he pay Robert because of that? Robert wondered what Albert would be like as a person to work for. Robert had also met Albert's wife and been unimpressed by her shrewish manner. Just how impatient would they be with a one-armed man? Robert had thought the job offer had been couched in grudging terms and had loathed the condescending tone of pity of the entire interview. He did wish he still had his arm. He had not been able to put the meeting out of his mind since it ended, and today he was aware that the brittleness of his temper had only increased as the morning progressed. He would have to crawl to keep that job. Did he want to?

Robert was now walking along the seafront. He was thinking of life before the war. He remembered the optimism he had felt. What had happened to that? He strode along, Pooky at his side – some of the time at least. Pooky was a cheerful mutt, because he was too stupid to know any better. When the dog came running back after chasing after some intriguing smell, Robert gave him a sly kick. Even Pooky's whimpering response, and the appealing look the dog gave him, evoked no sympathy. As far as Robert was concerned, the only thing the dog did right was run off again.

His sister had loved this daft mongrel, which only made Robert wonder what women understood about anything. When Robert thought of it, women annoyed him as much as dogs. He remembered those groups of teenage girls who had gone about giving white feathers to young men. They were just having a go at men as far as Robert could see, but the end result of it was that men felt honour-bound to go and enlist. They'd marched off to the sound of cheers and ended huddling in funk holes in trenches while bombs dropped all around them. All those fine, tall, straight-limbed young men had been brave enough, but flesh against shells always loses. They had fought and fallen, screaming in their death agonies. The ones who had been fortunate enough to return had come back as different men.

Those silly young women. Did they have any conception of what it was like to walk down a street with only one arm? You need two arms to have proper balance. Just the way Robert walked annoyed him. The way those children he was passing licked their ice creams and grinned, annoyed him. The brightly coloured deck chairs annoyed him. That young woman walking hand in hand with her two-armed boyfriend particularly annoyed him.

Robert thought of Helen and of the way she had finished with him. Robert would have thought women could have found it in them to give men some comfort after the hell they'd been through, but Helen had left him for her fine two-armed young fellow. Robert knew that man too. He was another one who had been declared unfit for combat and not seen a moment at the Front. Unfit? He was hale and hearty enough to take Robert's girl away from him. Robert hated Helen from the bottom of his heart for that.

Robert noticed the way the young woman in front of him was turning her face to her young man, as she laughed in a sickeningly carefree manner on her way onto the Ridges. Robert hated her too; he hated every young woman in the world these days.

* * *

The final punishment the army had given Frank Bywaters was still burned into his psyche. He had been tied with wire to posts with his arms and legs spread wide, close against the perimeter fence. If he so much as moved his head from one side to the other, the barbed wire cut into his face. This was called the crucifixion punishment and, having experienced it, Frank thought it well named. While he hung there, helpless, soldiers drilled and marched past him, swivelling their eyes right as they jeered at him to the orders of their sergeant. This was all because he did not want to kill anybody. He hated every one of those soldiers for that. What the army did to a man was dreadful, and there was no avoiding the army. He was called up to it whether he agreed or not. They told him that if a soldier disobeyed an order he could be shot, so that Field Punishment Number One, the crucifixion stance, was presented as a kind alternative. Just holding that position for hours was hell. Every muscle ached, and the shame of it filled him – this was where his noble ideals had led him. The army would make sure it broke those down. The company of other conscientious objectors might have helped but he had been isolated.

It was after this that Frank agreed to join the Non-Combatant Corps. He had discovered he did not have what it took to be an absolutist who would do nothing for the war effort, and the shame of that still inflamed him. He had let Clifford Allen and those other heroes down.

There had been so many punishments. The first form of protest that he and the other objectors had agreed on was to refuse to wear a uniform, but Frank had to give up on that. Soldiers manhandled him into it, hitting him with fists and boots when it suited them. He regretted lacking the stubbornness of others and just knowing he was not made of the same stern stuff made him bitter. An anger had grown in him, one that had been foreign to his nature but, once there, it had stayed, though he hid it as much as he could. His defeat by army discipline was not something he confessed to at home. He said that he had agreed to join the Non-Combatant Corps out of a feeling of patriotism, as he did not want to let down the men on the firing line. He would not kill, but that did not mean he would not help. This had been a large lie. He had broken down and begged to be allowed to join it, tears streaming down his face.

Daphne had said she admired him for the principled stance he had taken, for the strength and courage he had shown in his own way, and he knew he did not deserve that from her. He wished he had the strength of his convictions, but he did not. He had told himself he would not be part of the war in any way, and he had ended up working out of his skin to be exactly that. In losing his battle with the army, not only had his peace of mind been shattered, but also, to a great extent, his sense of self.

After the war had finished, what had he come back to? He loved teaching, even had a talent for it, but had lost any career prospects he might have had. He had been well thought of at the prestigious school he had taught in before he had been called up, and the headmaster had arranged to have him exempted from the war. All he had to do was go to the recruiting station, agree to join up, and be excused for essential work, but Frank would not agree. Frank was fired up with enthusiasm for the cause of conscientious objectors after going to their meetings and listening to the likes of Clifford. He wanted to make a stance. Now, that same school could not employ him because parents would object, and the school could not afford to lose good will.

Frank was reduced to helping out in a third-rate school, when they had need of him, in the mornings, with none of the job satisfaction of before and none of the prospects.

He was a discontented seething mess, and he knew it. He tired of his marking early and strode off to try to walk off his irritation. The boys could wait a bit before their English essays were returned to them. He hated the tensions he now suffered from. If he met up with any of the men who had jeered at him when he had been on his crucifixion stance, he would have killed any of them; so,

168

with murder in his heart, he let his feet find their way where they would – and it turned out to be towards the Ridges.

* * *

When Pulteney died for the murders I committed, I should have felt shame, but I'd given evidence against him and convinced myself there was no reason why his execution should concern me. I had meant to give up killing after that, as I had escaped scot-free. So, why put myself in danger from the police again? But murder was seductive, and I succumbed again. It was the anger that committed the murders and not me. That was what I told myself.

I testified against Pulteney not because he annoyed me in any way, but for self-preservation. I had even liked him. Something in him called to me. He had been in the same dark places that I had. That was why I understood his need to follow all those women. The lightness in the way their voices lilted compelled me as much as they did him, so I was not surprised now that I was again fascinated by the music in the voice of the woman who walked ahead of me. When she quarrelled with her young man and strolled further into the dunes, I followed her. I could not ignore that light sway to the hips and the spirited way she tossed her head.

Leaving Birtleby, in the way I had, should have worked. All that walking should have tramped the anger out of me, but it seemed to have distilled it into a rage even purer and more malevolent.

From spike to spike, I had tramped. I got to know some of the other gents of the road but never found companionship. Anger had left me in a lonely place. I thought back sometimes to what I had done to Pulteney. I had destroyed him. It had been necessary, but now, at this distance, there were the occasional pangs of regret. I had come to realise what Pulteney had been doing in those innocent walks of his, behind the voices of young women. He had been healing himself. He did not mean those women harm; he worshipped their femininity from his distance, and that was enough for him. That passion of his communicated itself to me. When I looked at those women through his eyes, it was as if I was seeing them myself for the first time, and I saw what Pulteney meant about their lightness and innocence. I felt

169

the need to protect that from what I had learned in the war. Was that really why I killed them? Strange the force that propelled me then. Love become anger and anger love, an inexplicable mix in my soul. Once someone was dead, they had no more to fear: that was my thinking. In the process, I also killed Pulteney. Something in me had gone wrong and I could not work it out. I did escape it for a time on my wandering, but I met it again when I returned to Birtleby. It seemed to have hovered somewhere above these sands, waiting for me to return and find it again.

Now, I was walking behind another young woman on the Ridges. Why was she drawing me with her into the dunes? Did she have no guilt about what she was doing to me? Those other young women had killed Pulteney in their own way. If they had not drawn him on, then I, Chris, would never have killed them, and Pulteney would not have been executed for it. And here I was, again behind another one of those beckoning young women.

I thought again of Pulteney dangling on his rope. That was a picture I could not stop returning to, as hard as I tried, not that I'd witnessed it. You didn't have to, in order to imagine that. Think of this moment now, I told myself — the give of sand under my feet, the rhythm in my limbs. There was warmth from the sun on my skin. The brightness of the sun as it glanced off the waters drew the eye. Everything was clear wherever I looked, the marram grass with its light sway in the breeze, the gull soaring above, and suddenly any thought of Pulteney had gone. It was as if there was something in this landscape I was recognizing for the first time.

But the anger still moved through me like a breeze; no, more like a wind, a wind from the north, driving all that coldness from there, as it gathered strength, blowing over miles of sea, a wind that blew and cut and demanded obedience from me.

I continued to follow her. Even from that distance, I could almost feel that animal softness to her skin. Why did she have to continue drawing me like that?

Then, something else blew in with that wind, a memory of the thunder of guns and the bite of bullets in the air. The ground heaved under my feet again, as if at the impact of shells. I heard a scream inside my head; that scream of pain from a fellow soldier had been echoed by a scream of pain inside myself.

CHAPTER TWENTY-THREE

Florence only just avoided the blow when it came. There was a movement of air beside her head which she turned away from in the nick of time to let a rock fly past her. Her body adopted a ju-jitsu stance and she turned to lean her body forward, hooking her right leg behind her assailant's legs while she pushed him over into the ground. She had said she could sit on any man and hold him down in agony, and she attempted to, as she twisted his arm straight behind his back into a lock position; but he heaved with his legs and suddenly the arm was freed, and Florence was levered over onto her back, her breath expelled with the shock of it. There was a physical strength, and a will here, that was overpowering. Then his weight was on her, as his hand gripped her throat and she was the one writhing.

Florence became aware of a rushing movement and an angry male voice. The hand was hauled away from her throat and she gulped at air. She tried to force her brain to work and take in what was going on around her.

Blades had hauled her assailant over into a prone position. Then Blades was kicked off and flew backwards, landing in a heap of objecting limbs. At that point,

Peacock materialised, a flying body with a right hook. The murderer now tumbled over as Peacock followed up with blows to the body. Then Peacock was kicked by a vicious lunge to the stomach, and he was on his knees coping with the pain of that.

Florence stretched out a leg to lever the man onto his back, then jumped on top of him to try to hold him but was kicked off with strong blows to her stomach and head, which sent her staggering.

Then Blades was back at the man and he had his truncheon out. He aimed it at the man's arm in an attempt to break it. But the truncheon was kicked out of his hand.

Florence blinked. This was a kicking, whirling demon with a face that seemed one great snarl. The man kicked out again and caught Peacock on the jaw as he lunged at him. Florence thought it would be a wonder if the jaw had not been broken. Now, Florence had her hand on Blades' truncheon and enjoyed the crunch as she drove it into the man's shoulder. He grunted. She hit him again, to the ribs this time, and he dropped to his knees. Then Blades was at him with two, three, four, five quick blows to the nose, followed by two to the stomach, and the man crumpled.

Peacock hauled out his handcuffs and slapped them round a wrist, then looked for another, but there wasn't one. It had taken all this effort to subdue a one-armed man. Peacock placed the other cuff round his own wrist, and snapped it shut.

Blades was struggling for breath but managed to blurt out with a note of relief as well as triumph, 'Robert Tanner, I am arresting you for the murders of Daphne Tanner, Jane Proudfoot, and the attempted murder of Florence Smithson, police constable. You do not have to say anything, but anything you do say will be written down with glee and definitely used in evidence against you.'

'Bastards,' Robert replied. 'Is no one allowed to hand out justice without the police interfering?'

'You'll find justice soon enough,' Blades said.

CHAPTER TWENTY-FOUR

Once Robert had started talking, they could not get him to stop. Blades wondered if he was boasting – or maybe he needed to get it off his chest.

'It was my hand that held the rock I killed Daphne with, but it didn't feel as if it was me doing it.'

'Really, sir?'

Robert looked into the distance and his eyes seemed to lose focus, before they hardened into the present again.

'I was livid with Helen, and that wasn't surprising. So, why did I take it out on Daphne?'

A good question, Blades thought, and one he would like the answer to. Robert chewed his lip, muttered something, then coughed. He pondered something for a moment or two, then seemed to reach a decision.

'It must have been what Daphne said when I told her. She told me to grow up. Grow up, I ask you. I hadn't even known she was on that stretch of beach. I wasn't expecting to come across her. It was a bit windswept and, I don't know, sort of wild, and it made me feel wild – maybe. That's an excuse. It was my temper. I lost control. And there isn't any undoing it. But it felt natural. It just happened. All by itself. Really. I was just so angry, with

Helen, and with Daphne, and Daphne was the one there. And there was that rock, and then it was in my hand. I just wanted some relief from all that tension, all that fury. And it worked. She fell over and I didn't connect that with me lashing out at first. But some of the anger had gone and seeing her lying there like that made me feel better. Then I realised I had done that. I felt – what you would expect. Why did I kill Daphne? She didn't deserve it. Then I realised I was going to hang for this, and I remembered where I was, and I tried to make it look like one of the Ridges murders. Or like they had been described in the press. But you don't understand any of that, do you?' he said to Blades.

'Try me, sir.'

'You couldn't. You weren't at the Front, were you? I remember reading that in a newspaper about you.'

'No. But what does that have to do with you murdering Daphne?'

'You don't get it. They all died, you know. Everybody you enlisted with, everybody you ate with, showered with, laughed with. They died. When they sent you over the top stumbling with all that ammunition and those weapons they made you carry, and you found yourself struggling through the mud and the bullets that cut down everyone around you, that's what happened. They all died. Except me. Why wasn't I killed? I should have been. Have you ever felt afraid? You think you have. But you haven't until you've been out there in that.

'Have you heard of the Blighty wound? The one that gets you your ticket home and away from it all? I longed for one of those.

'So, there I was. I'd survived the assault. I was back in a trench. But even that wasn't safe. They had snipers who tried to pick you out there too. Every dawn. You knew they were sitting there with their rifles ready to fire. I put my hand up and a bullet struck it. And that was that. My Blighty wound. I had made sure I wouldn't be killed out there, that I would be going home. I didn't know it could mean me losing my arm. And I'd stuck up the wrong one. I wasn't able to work as a tailor again when I returned. I didn't know I was coming back to being pitied and useless, and unable to tell anybody it was all my own fault. They wouldn't feel sorry for me then, would they? I wish I'd died out there instead.

'So, yes. I'm an angry, unhappy man. And I killed Daphne because of it. I wish I hadn't. I should have killed myself, shouldn't I? That would have been more sensible. Wouldn't it?'

Blades and Peacock could only sit and listen and gawp at the man in front of them.

'But to go on, to try to explain it to myself because I don't get it either. Helen had left me for a man with two arms. I was annoyed, and the feelings were strong ones, out of the depth of me, completely overpowering. I just seemed to slip back amongst all those bullets and shells, and the need to lash out and kill someone, anyone, so that I might survive. Then Daphne was lying on the ground beside me, and it was as if something had taken control of me and done it.'

'Is that what happened to Jane?' Blades asked.

'I suppose you do want to know about that. How to explain? I'd lost Helen and I'd lost Daphne. Jane had been keen on me once, so I thought I might have a go there. We arranged to meet up, but it was different. She wasn't interested. She'd only met up with me out of pity, and I didn't even deserve that. It was the knife that decided to kill her. It doesn't make sense otherwise.'

Good, thought Blades. Robert had confessed to the murder of Jane Proudfoot too. They would have him sign a statement to that effect as quickly as possible. But he could not stop himself criticising Robert for one thing he had said.

'No, sir. It wasn't the knife. You plunged it into Jane.'

'You're right, of course,' Robert said. 'It was me. I killed Jane.'

'We'll need a statement from you, sir.'

But the person in front of Blades had gone elsewhere. There was a vacant look on his face as if he had left anything rational behind him. Then he returned from wherever he had been.

'Of course,' he said.

CHAPTER TWENTY-FIVE

Frank did not know how to define his feelings when he was told that Daphne's murderer had been caught. He was pleased the killer was locked up, and glad to finally know the name of the murderer. It had been a question that had ached inside him: who could have done such a thing? But Robert, her brother? Frank knew Robert was a strange person, but it was difficult to come to terms with the fact that someone he knew so well could have done that. He supposed Robert had been destroyed by the war. It was the only thing approaching a defence that could be made. But killing Daphne?

Frank thought of his own feelings towards her. She had been the best thing in his life, indeed the only good thing since the war. He did not know how he would build his life again on his own. Frank thought of the way her hair caught the light, chestnut, springy, shining. It was so soft in the fingers too. Daphne, she with the eyes that shone, she with the quickest laugh, and the kindest smile. Daphne, the only one with patience for him. She was dead. He was finding it difficult to cope with that and supposed he would continue to.

It was only lately, now that he had been left on his own, that he had started to reconsider his own war. Had he been right to come out as a conscientious objector? When he considered the personal cost, he hoped so. The vilification had been dreadful, and he resented it, but he had to admit that he had singled himself out for it. The wonderful thing was that Daphne, who had done nothing to deserve it, had been prepared to go through it with him. It was dreadful what he had lost in Daphne.

He did regret not having the courage to be an absolutist. He was a half-and-half man, he thought. Serving in the brigade, he had wished he had the courage to be like some of the others. If you are going to be a conscientious objector, go all the way. But he was not without some pride. Killing was wrong, the point had to be made, and he had gone some way towards making it at least.

He had shown some strength of character if not as much as he would have liked, yet he was aware that his strengths were also weaknesses. Even if not stubborn enough to be an absolutist, he was, in most circumstances, too much so, and had too much intellectual conceit. He ought to be prepared to consider someone else's point of view now and again. And he needed to join in more. Even as a boy, he had not done that, but stuck out for what he felt like doing.

The war, though, was a factor that found many people wanting. Peace had been declared but still had to be found for many people – like him. How did he come to terms with anything?

He supposed he would. He just wished he had Daphne to help him.

* * *

It was in Birtleby that I found the worst of myself, and it was only by leaving there, that I left it behind. I had not meant to come back because I thought the killing might return too, which it almost did. I was tempted because the opportunity was there. Something in

*me managed to resist it but it is not something I am sure I can rely
on. I will have to leave Birtleby again. That anger is still inside me,
pretending to be my friend, walking with me all the way.*

*So, I do leave – in search of the peace of the road, but all that
tramping does not work. I cannot walk far enough to escape the
memories of those bodies lying on a beach. Then, it comes to me what
I can do about that.*

*I turn towards the waves and cast about on the beach for rocks
and stones. I fill the pockets of my overcoat with them. Then, I walk
into the sea. If I cannot walk out my anger, perhaps I can bury it,
and a sea burial will serve. I walk further out into the waves. The
water is cold but there is something soothing about that harshness. I
put one foot in front of another till the water is up to my waist.
Something sings in the ears and I hear it all again. The big guns
bellow, machine guns rattle, and lines of bullets spit around me.
Perhaps this time they will not miss. I do not want them to. I keep on
walking forward till the water is up to the neck. I pause, then put
another foot forward.*

* * *

When Chris's body was found during one of the
occasional very low tides, nobody associated it with the
Ridges murders. The body was much decomposed by then
and nobody even knew it had once belonged to Chris.
Robert had been hanged and Birtleby had returned to its
life, though there were always tales of some malevolent
spirit out there preying on youth, something left over from
the Great War and that had never quite finished with all
that destructiveness. Perhaps, that was the only way people
could ever come to terms with any of that – by turning it
into tales.

If you enjoyed this book, please let others know by leaving a quick review on Amazon. Also, if you spot anything untoward in the paperback, get in touch. We strive for the best quality and appreciate reader feedback.

editor@thebookfolks.com

www.thebookfolks.com

Two soldiers recently returned from WWI are accused of murdering a woman. They protest their innocence but are convicted on circumstantial evidence and given the death penalty. One of the soldiers begins to suspect the other as guilty. But can he betray his brother in arms who saved his life during the war?

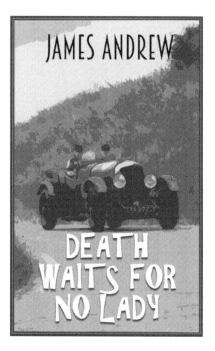

When a parlour maid finds her wealthy mistress dead,
Detective Blades is called in to investigate. The lady of the
house's lifestyle has changed considerably following the
death of her father, so the police focus on her many
apparent suitors. Which of them could have wanted her
dead?

Available on Kindle and in paperback from Amazon.

Printed in Poland
by Amazon Fulfillment
Poland Sp. z o.o., Wrocław

49706720R00113